For Alice —

The
Magic Stories

a collection by
Marie Sheppard Williams

Marie S. Williams

∞INFINITY
PUBLISHING

Copyright © 2012 by Marie Sheppard Williams
Cover art and cover design by Megan Williams
Author's photo by Megan Williams

ISBN 978-0-7414-7280-9

Printed in the United States of America

This is a work of fiction. Names, characters, places, and incidents either are the product of the author's imagination or are used fictitiously. Any resemblance to actual events or locales or persons, living or dead, is entirely coincidental.

Published April 2012

INFINITY PUBLISHING
1094 New DeHaven Street, Suite 100
West Conshohocken, PA 19428-2713
Toll-free (877) BUY BOOK
Local Phone (610) 941-9999
Fax (610) 941-9959
Info@buybooksontheweb.com
www.buybooksontheweb.com

"...tender stories...deliciously simple dialogue...sly humor...and you suddenly know you are reading about life and death."
—Howard Zinn, author of *A People's History of the United States.*

"....fine second book....direct, colloquial, truthful, and full of the music of ordinary speech... As Walt Whitman might have said: 'Who touches this book touches a [wo]man."—Bill Holm, Minnesota author and poet.

The God Stories—(Fire Tree Press, 2006)

The God Stories is marvelous. Marie Sheppard Williams does what Emily Dickinson does: she watches the back yard closely and notices the cosmos circling....by the end of the story, life has grown larger and more complicated—as it should in good stories.
—Bill Holm, Minnesota author.

["Jeanie 49 Duluth" is] an amazing, heartbreaking, and inspiring story by Marie Sheppard Williams....This story was so good, I'd buy any journal where Sheppard Williams appears in the Table of Contents. — From a review in *The New Pages Literary Magazine Reviews.* ("Jeanie 49 Duluth is included in *The God Stories*.)

Us—(Infinity Publishers)
....another wonderful book.—Dave Wood

The Best Cat—
Attention cat lovers!
Get with it and buy the latest effort by one of my favorite authors, Marie Sheppard Williams, and her daughter, Megan Williams. They've collaborated on a very charming book called "The Best Cat" (Infinity Publishing, $9.95). —Dave Wood, syndicated columnist.

To Myrtle Clara Coplen
a magician
who taught me whatever
I know about
magic

and to Megan

CONTENTS

Acknowledgements

I want to thank Diane Smith, the publisher of *Grey Sparrow,* who first published "Marty" in the online version of her magazine.

I also want to thank all the people who, over years, read and critiqued these stories; and Donna Jansen and Liza Lawrence, who proofread these stories.

Author's Preface

Magic. Why do I call these stories *magic stories?* Well. Because all the stories involve magic in one form or another.

Now you'll want to know how many forms there are. Oh, lots. Plain old magic—black and white. Black with bad intentions, white with good. Voodoo. Witchcraft. Prayer. It's all the same. It all taps into an area of knowledge that has nothing to do either with the intellect, or with what appears to be sensible.

That's what *I* think, anyway.

I don't know or do much magic, but what little I do know I mostly learned from a blind social worker named Myrtle Clara Coplen. She taught me, for example, to throw the magic circle— well, it can be any shape really, just so it surrounds the person you are trying to keep safe. My personal magic circle looks like a doughnut, or a fat, sparkly hula hoop. Myrt's was like a big egg.

Myrt taught my daughter Megan, big-time learning-disabled, to read when she was fourteen. Megan was headed straight for jail or the bin at that time, and now she is an architect with her own firm in London. Surely that's a kind of magic too.

I think so.

Myrt wouldn't let me watch the reading lessons.

One day Megan said to me when she was a little kid: Isn't it amazing? I just let my bike lay on the lawn and nobody ever steals it.

That's because I put the magic circle around it, Megan, I said.

I don't believe in that kind of crap, said Megan.

Okay, I'll take the circle off, I said.

And twenty minutes later the bike was stolen.

Megan still half-way believes that Mum—that's British for *Mom,* you know, Megan is now more of a Brit than she is an American—anyway, she still sort of believes that Mum can do magic.

Put a magic circle around me, Mum, she'll say when she's going into an exceptionally difficult presentation.

So I do—when I remember. What the hell, it certainly can't hurt, can it?

And maybe—just maybe—it can do good.

Open your eyes. Look around you. Believe. There's magic everywhere.

Once a numerologist said to me: *First* you believe and *then* the miracles start to happen....

I don't know, it seems to me that life is just more fun when you believe.

Right at this very moment, I have a beautiful silver and stone talisman buried in my front yard; I'll dig it up at full moon— today—after Mother Earth has cleansed it of all the anger that was in it. Then I'll let it lie on top of the earth overnight in the full moon, and then for a day in the sun.

Be sure you mark the spot, said Teesie, who helped me to do this.

I've spent hours digging to find something I've buried. Teesie said.

See? More fun.

I mean, what are *you* doing at this very moment that's this much fun?

THE FOURTH HOUSE

I had this strange, strange dream, this very wonderful dream, about ten years ago when I was going to art school, at MTI and when Connor and Lace and I were students together. God: I was fifty-one years old at the time and I was going to art school, can you believe it?—when I went to the bank to apply for my student loan the clerk said: "Is this for you?" I mean she was *incredulous*, an old lady like me? and I wanted to say, Certainly it's for me, dummy; but I didn't, all I really said was: Yes.

Yes, it was for me. Going to art school was absolutely and definitively *for me*. The loan—which I am still paying back—was *for me*. Yes.

Anyway: the dream.

There is a house, a huge, rambling old mansion with three or four floors. On the top floor there is a sort of rummage sale going on, and I see things from different parts of my life, and all these things have price tags on them, cheap, they are all going cheap. I see the stuffed alligator that Holly Shaw bought years ago—at the Vassar rummage sale, the classiest rummage sale in town, if you can think of a rummage sale as being classy at all, why, you actually had to *pay* to get in. In the dream the alligator is marked ten cents, which as a matter of fact is what Holly did pay for it, if I remember right.

I saw a lamp made of genuine camel skin, or so the tag claimed, painted in vivid colors that became luminescent when the lamp was lit; it made an ordinary room seem like an Aladdin's cave. Vange and I gave that lamp to the CRS secretary when she got married. That was maybe twenty years ago when I was first working at the local center for blind people, and Vange was a blind social worker. I suppose that lamp is in an attic somewhere now, God, no one would actually *use* such a lamp. Well: not *no one*: I would have used it. Vange would have. And Vange did get one for herself later on: she still has it in her house on Aldrich Avenue South: you will hear more about that later.

Anyway, there is the lamp in my dream, marked two dollars.

CRS, in case you were wondering, stands for Community Rehabilitation Services, which I was manager of almost ten years, until I quit to go to art school.

But back to the dream. I do tend to wander around, and you could think that it's because I'm getting older, but it isn't, it's because I'm me. I have always been this way. In my mind, one thing leads to another, always. All connected. Everything. Anyway: the dream. There was a Persian carpet that I remember from my grandmother's house on Second Street. There was the set of doll furniture that I made years ago for my ex-husband's niece—practically everything in my life is ex by now—with a little hand-made mattress, tufted just so cunningly, what a joy that mattress was to me, I hated to give it away.

There is my old teddy bear, which I still have, dear old bear. My first doll. My grandma's portrait. A star for the Christmas tree that I had in my first apartment when I went to college. Clothes that I remember: my high school graduation dress, lemon-yellow cotton; my confirmation dress; my brown and white dress from kindergarten that my Aunt Ruth gave me; a little Chagall print smock I made for my daughter Margaret when she was a baby. Etc., etc., etc. On and on. Piled on tables in the dream. Beads and books and bracelets. Cups. Shoes and ships. Sealing wax.

Cabbages.

Kings.

(You know what this is, don't you? Why, this is a *catalog*, isn't it, like Homer used in the Iliad? For example. And that came to be a standard in other classical poetry. Can you detect that I was once an English major?—*We know what we are*, etc. A catalog is a list. A list of different kinds of trees, e.g. This is a list of old junk. A life list.)

You may choose to come in by the front door of this house— in my dream— and walk up several flights of stairs to get to the rummage sale.

Or, alternatively, you can come in another way, around the back, and enter the sale without climbing any stairs.

But built in a row leading into the back of the house at the rummage sale level are four much smaller houses. They are strung out, end to end, and the front of one is the back of the next: you have to go through each of the small houses to get to the next one, and through all of them to get into the big house.

The first small house is called The Hidden House. The second is The Secret House. The third is The Magic House.

The fourth house—the last—has a name, but no one knows what it is. I wake up not knowing.

I keep trying to remember the name of the fourth house. It seems so important. It seems to me that I knew it once and have now forgotten it. I wake from sleep sometimes—even now, ten years later—clutching at the tag-end of that name, God, I can almost see it, I can almost speak it with my mouth, the Dum-de-dum House—you know?—I almost have it, but never quite, you know how that is?

Maddening, that's how it is. There is a big secret, and I am not quite in on it.

And in the dream Connor and Lace and I, hand in hand, walk into the first little house: The Hidden House.

That's all. That's the end. I wake up.

*

Lace. That's an actual girl's name. Well, in a way; Lace was christened Leslie Ann, but no one at the school knew that except me. And maybe Connor.

Why *Lace*? I said to her one day. I mean, I like it, don't misunderstand me, I think it suits you perfectly, but—

Well: said Lace. It's really Leslie Ann. My Mama is from Kentucky and she talks with an accent and she always called me, like, *Lacely*, kind of like, when I was a child, and my little brother shortened it to Lace and...I liked it. I kept it.

Lace is perfect, I said. Lace. Just right.

Lace laughed. Full of holes? she said, in this slow, slow voice that she had, sweet, like honey pouring, full of laughter, even when things were totally grim: a kind of gray and anxious laughter.

Not full of holes, I said. Graceful. Gentle. Good. Old-fashioned. Delicate. Beautiful.

Oh, go *on*, said Lace. You must be blind. You must be crazy.

I knew she was pleased that I said that, though. Her face went all pink: so pretty with her gray eyes and her halo of blond curls.

No, I said. I'm not blind. I'm not crazy. I see what is there. It's my personal catastrophe, I said. I always see.

*

I do see, you know. Some people do.

How come you know so many nuts: said Holly Shaw one time when I was describing someone I knew: you remember Holly, she is the one who bought the alligator at the Vassar rummage sale.

Actually, now that I am thinking about it, it may have been a small crocodile.

It was a real stuffed skin, too, not a cloth toy. About two feet long. A baby. Nowadays I think you couldn't find such an item, alligators and crocodiles being on protected lists as endangered species.

Well, I don't, I said to Holly. Know so many nuts. I just know so many ordinary people awfully well.

And that's it, you know. Scratch an ordinary person deep enough, you'll find a nut. Almost every time.

I thought of writing a story about Holly; years and years ago this was; but the title was going to be "Ordinary People," and before I could write it someone else took that title. I'll never write it now; without that title I can't get up any enthusiasm for the project. Enthusiasm—you know that means? From the Greek— entheos: full of God.

*

Connor and Lace and I pretty much drifted together by default. It just happened, as these things mainly do just happen. For one thing, everybody else was much younger than the three of us: mostly they were about eighteen or nineteen years old. Up to maybe twenty-five. Twenty-six. Something like that. Grady was maybe thirty, he was married and had kids; but he was the exception. Nobody else except me and Lace was married. And except me and Grady, nobody else had kids: I had a daughter, but she was grown up, no longer in my life in any day-to-day way.

Connor and Lace were both about thirty-five, I'd guess, though I never really asked them, I never really knew; and me, I told you before how old I was.

Grady, that I mentioned before: he was an exception to everything. He belonged with nobody. He was almost always by himself. Well, though, this was inevitable: he had the most talent. Everybody else was leagues behind him—even me, and I was very good.

But Grady was simply terrific.

They shouldn't let people like him in here, little Gayle complained: he's had art training already, he told me so.

It isn't fair, she said. To the rest of us.

What art training? I said.

He took the whole Famous Artists' Course, she said. By mail. When he was just out of high school. And he sells things. I mean, he's a professional already, what is he doing here...

God. What were any of us? Doing? There?

*

And the Famous Artists' Course: my goodness. Gracious.

*

Gayle—*little* Gayle, four feet ten—was a failed barber: she had taken the complete barbering course, ten months, also at MTI, which was the school we were all going to for commercial art: Minneapolis Technical Institute. That's what it was called then. I understand they've changed the name recently. I guess they are trying to tart it up, make it more classy, the words *technical* and *institute* have I guess no intellectual status. Unless it's MIT. Maybe. The word *Minneapolis* is still okay. It's still the *Minneapolis* Something Or Other. But a rose by any other name: no matter how you cut it: is still a vo-tech, and not a college. It is not for example the Minneapolis College of Art and Design: MCAD, the local Cadillac of art schools. Em-cad, you pronounce it.

Em-cad.

*

Why did you stop being a barber, Gayle? I asked her.

There was too much stress, she said.

Stress? I said. Being a *barber?*

Well, people wouldn't like their haircuts, she said. Sometimes. They would get mad. I was always afraid.

Fear flicked in her eyes, alive still, at the memory.

*

Pretty Kim was right out of high school. She had a little talent. Enough. Her aunt was one of the teachers in the art department at MTI. So her coming to the school was just in the nature of things: natural.

*

Amy and Brian and Georg—Georg was a transplanted Latvian—wanted to be photographers. But the photography sequence was part of the commercial art course, and you couldn't take it separately. So they struggled with the art classes to get the photography. They had no gift for art at all, they had a terrible time with the drawing and painting. But they were terrific at photography. And little by little they learned something about art. Actually, I was eventually amazed to realize how good they became with almost no native ability.

*

None of these people matter a great deal here—you can pretty much forget about them now, they are not important to this story; they have their own stories, I imagine they do—but I have put them in here just to give you a feeling for all the people who were in the school with us. There were seventeen of us in all.

*

(Why *was* Grady there? No one had any clue. I mean, he knew it all already, he knew more than the teachers did, so why was he there? People are so damned remarkable when you really look at them, aren't they?—I mean, they do the damnedest things and you hardly ever know why.)

*

Connor Sheahy was a funny, gossipy little man, Irish of course, Black Irish he said, short, only a little taller than me, and I am five feet four. In a way he was almost a dwarf, because he had a large head and a disproportionately muscular upper body and suddenly below the waist very slim hips and legs. He had black, lank hair and a skimpy black mustache, and he almost always wore a black leather beaked cap; that cap made him look faintly sinister, like a little hood, but an amateur one.

He came from a small town in Wisconsin, where his family still lived: a mother, about whom one heard very little, and a young sister Maureen, still in high school: Maureen, I thought, must have come as quite a surprise for the family, she must have been at least sixteen years younger than Connor; and Connor's father, who was a nurse in a hospital in that town.

Amazing, I said to Connor once, that your father chose to be a nurse: I mean, it must have been a very unusual choice for a man in that generation. Yeah, well: Connor said.

And in fact he never seemed comfortable talking about his family; let's talk about something else, he would say, I want to get shut of that town....

Connor worked as a waiter a couple of nights a week at La Tortue, which was the fanciest restaurant in Minneapolis at that time. Or one of the fanciest: it kind of cramped their style, though, when turtles went on the endangered list and they couldn't serve turtle soup any more. La Tortue: that's The Turtle. In French. You probably knew that.

Hey, Con, why are you in school? I asked him once.

Oh, god! he shouted: this is my *ticket out*! Are you *kidding? This is my passport to another life....*

*

We were all in school together for two years, and our teachers said that we were the best class they'd ever had at MTI. There were five or six of us who were really good, me and Grady and Leandra and Dennis and Little Gayle, and you could I guess count Lace, she was good but she could never finish anything. She fell farther and farther behind the rest of us. What she did do, was perfect, was just great, couldn't have been better. Well. Not Van Gogh, but you know what I mean.

You would think that with so many people at the top there would have been a lot of competition, but there wasn't any. We didn't compete, we helped each other. And the ones on top helped the slower ones.

Everybody helped poor old Lace. She couldn't make decisions, that was her main trouble: not about the simplest things, like what colors to use, what kind of brush to buy. What size paper. Like that. We made decisions for her.

Connor could have used some help too, but he was so independent, he absolutely had to do it all his own way. And *his way* was a little—well: weird—sometimes. He just listened to his own drum and did exactly what he wanted to do, no matter what the assignment was. Connor went his own way. Always. Independent, absolutely.

My father said to me once, *Joan, you're a good woman, but you're as independent as a hog on ice.* So who am I to talk about Connor?

The teachers commented on all this: they said we had a class neurosis, that we were all too nice, too humble, that we had no killer instinct.

They said that—in general—we'd never amount to a hill of beans. You have to have killer instinct, I guess, to amount to a hill of beans.

*

I told Connor and Lace about my dream the day after I had it. I had the most interesting dream, I said. You were both in it. And told them.

Gosh, Connor said, staring at me with what I think was admiration: that's a really crazy dream. Really weird.

And he laughed. That's what I like about you, Joan, you're really weird. He said. And laughed: this almost falsetto laugh that he had, like a flute: hah-hah-hah...

He took his paint-dipped brush off the project he was working on and waved it at me. A drop of paint splashed onto his work. Con always filled his brush too full, I was always telling him.

Thanks, Connor, I said. And the same to you.

Damn it, he said.

About the drip.

Lace was silent for a few seconds, I guess thinking about the dream: slowly and carefully, as she did everything. Then: It's a wonderful dream, she said. It's a dream from God.

What do you think the fourth house is, Lace? I said.

Maybe it's death, she said.

I shivered. Goose crossing your grave, Joan? said Connor.
He giggled: really. Observant; he was, you know. Always
watching: the littlest things.

How could it be death? I said. You don't go through death to
get to life. And the sale is my life, I'm sure of it.

Going cheap, cheap, CHEAP! Connor yelled, waving his
brush again, and dripping on the work table.

Heads all over the room turned toward the back three cubicles
where Connor and Lace and I had our tables. Hey, keep it down,
Connor, I said: You're disturbing the *artistes*.

Oh, pooh, said Connor. *I* am an *artiste*. These people are
hacks.

You can see why the other people in the class were not
altogether crazy about Connor.

If your mother dies, said Lace.

What? I said.

She said: That would be going through death into life...sort
of...if somebody died because you were born....

Did your mother die, Lace? I said. Quite gently. People did
speak gently to Lace, as if she could tear or break easily.

No...Lace said: slowly. But she will. Some day.

Connor stared at her.

You're very weird too, Lace, he said. You are both *very
weird*. He laughed again, that fluting laugh.

And Lace laughed too. Talk about the pot, she said.

Calling the kettle black....

*

Actually, I believe Connor did see himself as an artist, and all
the rest of us as commercially-motivated hacks. He was crazy
about the work of Henri Matisse, especially the cutouts Matisse
did toward the end of his life, when he was too crippled with
arthritis to paint any more; Connor loved those paper cutouts, and
was mad for swirls and curves and paisley shapes.

As far as my own opinion is concerned, I think Con had no
talent at all—what he had was a terrible desire, a terrible need to
be talented.

One day Connor said: *my lover*: and then we knew for sure
that Connor was gay: which we had sort of almost known all
along, but not exactly, if you know what I mean.

9

My lover came in and cleaned my apartment yesterday while I was at school, he said: I was so mad.

Gee, why? I said: I'd think that would be kind of nice. I wish somebody would come in and clean my house.

We were sitting, Connor and I, at a table in the common space at the school having early morning coffee and rolls. Con lived just across Loring Park and he got to school early every day, at eight o'clock or so, for breakfast, and I made it once in a while when I caught an early bus. I made a special effort to get there on Thursdays, because on Thursdays they had these fabulous caramel nut rolls, incredibly large, and drenched in caramel, *jeweled* with pecans, and for only one buck. Yum, yum.

Lace never got there early. Well, Lace never even got to the eight-thirty class on time. Nobody expected it any more.

It wasn't nice at all, said Connor firmly.

To have the apartment cleaned, he meant: we are back to that now.

It was a *criticism*, he said.

Of *me*.

I guess you could see it that way, I said. If you wanted to.

What's your lover's name, I said.

Stanton, he said. Stan.

And he's not my lover any more, he said: I broke up with him.

Because of the *cleaning?* I said.

Yes, he said. Well, no, actually that was the last straw.

He tossed his head: I-don't-give-a-damn.

There's plenty of fish in the ocean, he said.

*

The three of us, Connor and Lace and I, were a strange combination. We had, in the ordinary way of things, hardly anything in common. As I said in the first place, we came together by default—we were the three who were left when everybody else had found a niche.

And yet. There was something that held us together beyond the mere fact that we were in school. I can't tell you what the bond was. When I try to figure it out, I draw an absolute blank. But when I feel my way into it, I know that I loved them, and I believe that they loved me, and loved each other, in a funny sort of way.

We had no life together outside of school. I did not know their other friends; and—except for Vange that I mentioned early on, and I will tell you later how that happened, if you hang in with me I will eventually tell you everything; this is my *way*, meandering around like this is *my way*—anyway, except for Vange, Lace and Connor did not know my friends.

I had no particular wish to introduce them to my friends, either, which is unusual; you know how you meet a new person, and you like them, and you say: gosh, So-and-So would absolutely *love you*: and you trot the person off to meet old So-and-so, and they hate each other? well, that didn't happen here; I kept Lace and Connor separate.

The three of us together—I never think of us any other way, in the school connection it was like we were born again into a fourth fused entity—the three of us were like the Three Musketeers. Drei Kameraden. Or maybe—god, yes!—the three stooges. We were always together during class hours, we took care of each other, protected each other, felt loyalty and affection: acknowledged faults but accepted one another. And yet it was a loose loyalty, a loose affection: we made no demands at all on each other. And if anyone else had wanted to come into our little enclave, that would have been perfectly okay.

*

Did I tell you about Leandra? I think I told you that she was one of the really good artists. Well, Leandra kind of loosely belonged with me and Connor and Lace. She had come into the class about a month after it started, a transfer from a school in San Francisco; and you know how that is, when you come in late, unless you are an awfully strong personality, a natural leader, and you just *take over*, you never quite belong. Never entirely.

Leandra never quite belonged. But if she belonged anywhere at all, it was with me and Connor and Lace. Like I said: loosely.

One day we got an assignment in our media class: to write a script and make a story-board suitable for presenting—to a potential employer—an idea for a half-hour TV program. We were supposed to get into groups of four, I guess to teach us how to work with other people, a commendable goal, although personally I have never seen a job that couldn't be done better by one person alone. And faster, usually.

Well, I thought; sure; me and Connor and Lace and Leandra, that's a group.

But Leandra said no—to me, off privately in a corner when I tracked her down. But why? I said.

Lace is too unreliable, Leandra said. I don't want to work with Lace.

God, you know, the truth is I felt the same way. About then I was beginning to get mad at Lace for always being late, for being slow and undependable, for saying she'd do things and then not doing them; I wished I could be in another group too. And not with Connor either; when you came right down to it, what the hell could Connor *do*?

Here is a confession: there is a piece of me—still, after all this time and all these years of presumably learning something—a piece of me that has Killer Instinct.

Leandra had a lot of Killer Instinct. She was a very, very good artist and she had K.I.; the combination is unbeatable; and the fact is, after we graduated, Leandra was the only one of us who got a really good job right away—in fact, she had to start two weeks before our last classes were over—and she is an honest-to-god art director right now and travels all over the world. The last time I tried to call her, she was in Hong Kong. So you see they were right about K.I.

We haven't got four in our group, I said to Connor.

Sure we have, he said: Leandra.

Taking it for granted, just as I had.

Leandra won't, I said. Leandra is going in with Gayle and Dennis and Grady.

But! Connor said. Outraged. Why?

Because of Lace, I said. She doesn't want to work with Lace.

(Or you, Con, probably, I could have said.)

Well, said Connor: I can understand that.

Can't you? he said.

Yeah, I said.

In fact—said Con—maybe I should go with another group too. Maybe this is the time to *break out*.

Connor had had this notion for a while that he should broaden his school participation. I'll never be in school again, he said: I want to feel the old School Spirit, hang with the guys...

Like you were at Harvard, I said.

Oh, *yes*, said Connor, and sang: *We are poor...little lambs...that have lost...our way...baa, baa, baa....*

That's Yale, Con: I said.

Whatever, he said.

But he made a point for a while of going with the other students to a bar after classes to hang out.

You're too old, I told him. For them.

Grady goes sometimes, he said; why not me?

I could have told him, but what the hell?

It didn't take long before he came back to me and Lace. We took him back: again, what the hell. Not enough K.I.—that's the whole thing.

Maybe that's the whole thing.

And maybe it's not.

*

You can't go with another group: I said to Connor. You can't do that to Lace.

Connor looked astonished.

Of course I can, he said: I can be as selfish as the next person. I can choose for *me*. He stuck his tongue out at me.

I laughed at him, but: Not this time, Con, I said.

I *can*, he insisted. Certainly I can.

You can't, Con, I said. Think about it.

Suddenly he looked quite cross, and shook his head, baffled.

Why can't I? he said. Why can't I do things that are just for me? What's the matter with me?

You haven't got it in you, Con, I said. You're kind, that's the trouble.

You can't help it any more than you can help being short. Or gay. Or Irish.

I suppose you had to say *short*, he said. Terribly cross, he was.

How come you know so much? he said. Cross as a *bear*. Dear old Con.

I only know what's true, I said.

I told you, I said: I see things.

*

13

I guess it's about time I told you something about me, and how I happened to be in art school at the age of fifty-one. Better late than never: to tell you about me, I mean. And, now that I am thinking about it, also to go to art school.

My mother was still alive then, when I decided to go to school; she was living in her hi-rise apartment in North Minneapolis, which is where I grew up: on the north side of Minneapolis, on 44th and Sheridan.

And I was a social worker at the Center for the Blind—as I told you before, a manager.

One day my mother said to me: Is there anything in your life that you really regret?

My Mama was an interesting old lady: she seemed very simple, almost simple-minded, but she kept coming up with these startling thoughts, out of the blue.

Once, for example, she said to me: I think your whole life has been a search for a mother.

Well. I nearly choked.

But: Certainly not, I said: I've got you, haven't I?

And that was the end of that. Closing a gaping wound with a Band-Aid: that's me. No wonder I quit being a social worker. Denial is my middle name.

But sometimes I think that the greatest capacity of the human mind is denial. When it comes right down to it, what else have any of us got?—We are all going to get old, like it or not; we are all going to die.

Anyway, we hope so. Those of us with any sense at all.

*

Vange, the blind social worker I told you about earlier, always said: there's a lot more to your mother than you admit.

Yeah, yeah, Vange, I always said. And—basically—pooh, pooh. Not to mention: Mind your own business. You know how it is: you can see anybody else, but you can never see yourself: except in rare flashes, twenty years later: called illuminations. Epiphanies. Insights. These seem mostly to be negative—a matter of "accepting yourself." You hardly ever hear of anybody having a positive insight: *My word, I'm a saint*. No, it's always: *Oh, Christ, I'm a really terrible person, a human being like everybody else, and I have got to learn to accept it.*

But what did I *regret*? I really thought carefully about it, it was such a good question. Then: Well, I said, I think...the only thing I *really* regret...is that I didn't go to art school...

She looked disappointed, I thought. What had she hoped to hear?—I regret that I never knew you, Mama? I regret that you could never speak? or that I never could? I regret that I could not be the right kind of daughter for you? Some things are too damn deep for regret. I'll stick with what I can handle: I regret that I never went to art school.

*

So then of course I had to go to art school. I didn't go at the logical time in my life because I was scared. I mean, I made up a lot of reasons, but *that* is the truth: I was scared. Also my mother didn't want me to go to art school: you can't make a living as an artist, she said.

Look at Bernard, she said.

Bernard was her youngest brother, my uncle. Bernard started out to be an artist, but then he married Aunt Rhea and the kids started coming and he stopped being an artist and went to work in a leather factory in Detroit and worked there until he retired: forty-five years later.

And I had a problem with my eyes. An ophthalmologist in town, Dr. Elton, who was supposed to be the best, told me when I was eleven that I had progressive myopia and if I didn't stop reading so much and doing fine pen and ink art work I'd be blind by the time I was twenty. He was wrong about all of it, the diagnosis *and* the prognosis, but that was in my mind and it was another reason that I didn't become an artist.

But all these reasons, true as they were, were extra: the real reason was what I said: I was scared.

I went to the University of Minnesota instead, because my friends were doing that and I just sort of slipped in there with them. And I won a scholarship, kind of accidentally, I mean, to me it felt like it had just dropped from the sky.

Before that, I hadn't thought of going to college at all: girls didn't, in my family.

The scholarship was an English Club scholarship, so I figured I had to major in English, and that's what I did and here I am today, folks, writing a story about art school. It all feels accidental in one way, and like everything coming together as it had to, in another way.

Also, why—when I had the chance, or took it—did I go to MTI instead of MCAD? Because I never had a dream, like Connor did, of "being an artist": my dream, when I got out of high school, was of learning to do art and make a living: commercial art. And if you are making up for the thing you most regret, you must do it exactly as you dreamed it. Otherwise it won't be any good. You can see that.

Also, I knew that I had no real gift as an artist. I had talent in my hands—I can master any technique there is—but in the eye and in the head and the heart I didn't have it. And the eye and the head and the heart are where the real art is.

I never did use my MTI training, which was excellent, by the way, I thought; I never used it to make a living; I discovered somewhere along the way that I didn't want to do that after all, that I didn't want to work at art.

But I have turned out some kind of artist after all, as good as many. I draw and paint quietly for myself in a little studio I've fixed up in the basement of my house. And being an artist *for yourself*—that's pretty much where it's at, isn't it? When you think about it? Maybe Connor was an artist too, from that point of view.

*

Connor and Lace and I ended up as a three-person group for the media project, since by the time everything got sorted out, there was nobody left to join us.

We did all right on the project, too; in fact, we got an A-plus, probably the only one Connor or Lace ever got in the whole two years of school; we got it because I did my thing, which is to say I took over and ordered people around, portioned out tasks, set up meetings, and what-have-you. When I was a manager, I was a good one, as managers go.

I told Connor he could do the drawing: I mean, of all the things he couldn't do well, that one seemed to me to have the lowest potential for actual damage: who really knows these days whether bad drawing is accidental or on purpose?

I told Lace that she could do the final revision and typing and preparation of the script, and I made her promise that she would do it according to a time schedule that I gave her. I made the time schedule especially rigorous, because I was sure that come hell or high water she would have to be a *little* late, and this way it wouldn't hurt us.

Also, if worse came to worse, either Connor or I could type the script.

You are terribly bossy, Connor said, admiring.

Yes, I said.

You'd make a good *maitre de*, he said.

And to crown it: since I nominated myself to write the script, there wouldn't *be* any revisions to make at the end.

And I chose the subject of the project: well, I didn't exactly choose it, I just made it seem so attractive that Connor and Lace grabbed onto it in a minute. Some people would say that I rammed it down their throats; I say they swallowed it quite happily. Democracy in action.

(I have this fantasy about the members of the first Congress of the USA writing the Constitution: they are all squabbling like crazy and Tom Jefferson comes in with a bull-horn: NOW HEAR THIS...he roars.)

*

The project I came up with was a natural. Do you recall that I told you earlier in this story about Vange, who worked with me at the Center for the Blind? Well, just at that time Vange got fired; the administration put it as an invitation to take early retirement for the good of the agency; but everybody knew what it really was. And Vange refused to cooperate: No way, she said. If you want to fire me—she said—you have to tell people what you did. I'm not going to make it easy for you.

But! For the good of the agency! the director said. If I was doing something for the good of the agency, she said, I'd stay.

And you'd admit that, Gregory Roger, if you had any decency. Said Vange.

*

So anyway, Lace and Connor and I interviewed Vange for our project. Lace and Connor liked Vange a lot, got on with her like a house-afire. Well, but most people do like Vange.

And Vange liked them. I knew she would. In fact, she invited us all to lunch at her house. Vange is a wonderful cook, lunch at her house is really an occasion.

*

Lace was getting into deeper and deeper trouble in school. There was the problem with finishing things, but there was also the fact that her attendance was simply terrible. She stayed home a lot, and her reasons for doing so were never altogether convincing: she had a lot of funerals to go to, and her truck broke down a lot. For example.

Oh—Jerry had to use the truck yesterday, she would say.
Me: You couldn't take the bus?
Her: Yes, but:
The weather was too bad....
It would take so long: it wouldn't be worth it....
Jerry needed me to go with him....
Jerry's grandmother died.

Jerry was Lace's husband. He had been in Vietnam, and apparently there were residual problems. He was for example an alcoholic. Maybe a drug addict too. In any case, he had just got into AA, which, if there's anybody left in the world any more who doesn't know, is Alcoholics Anonymous.

In any case, Lace apparently spent a lot of time supporting Jerry around this attempt at recovery.

I know how it is, she said. I smoked pot for sixteen years. My god, I said: how did you get off of it? *Did* you get off of it?

Yes, I got off of it, she said. I just decided to stop one day about five years ago. I didn't go to AA or anything, or Narcotics Anonymous, I just quit.

Well, good for you, Lace, I said. That's amazing. But sixteen years! I'm surprised you didn't wreck your brain....

I think about that sometimes, she said. I worry about that. If my mind has been affected.

What do you think, Joan?

People at the school thought I was an infallible source of information on mental health questions, because I had been a social worker.

Gee, I don't know, I said. How would I know?

I don't think so, she said: I was always slow. My mother was always onto me about it: Lacely, she would say, how come you can't speed up a little here?

But I couldn't, Lace said.

My Mama is very good at things, Lace said. She's very fast. It seems as though she can do anything.

*

Lace told me that she and Jerry had been bikers together for a long time. Lace! I said: You were a biker-girl! Did you have your own bike?

No, she said, I rode behind Jerry.

Did you have a black leather jacket?

Well, sure, she said. We all did...

I can see it, I said: god, a biker-girl. And I could, you know: see it. I could see Lace as a young, young girl, riding post behind a big, bearded guy, her all soft and delicate, with her blond hair streaming out behind...in a leather jacket...high as a kite....

I loved it, she said. We had a Harley. I felt like somebody so special then...on the bike...with Jerry....

Why did you give it up, Lace?

Well, I don't know, she said: One day we just stopped. One day it didn't seem like such a good thing to do any more....

Two of our friends got killed in a crash, she said: there was a double funeral.

Jerry, when I met him years later, after we had graduated and were out in the world again, turned out to be a slender, rather fragile-looking man. He did have a beard, though. I wasn't wrong about that.

*

Once Lace was gone for a whole week. Me and Connor were determined to ignore it, we had heard so much about dying and dead friends and grandmothers and what-have-you, that we were, if you want to know the truth, kind of fed up.

But I couldn't hold out. After a week I called her.

Lace, I said: what's going on? We've missed you. Everybody's asking about you....

Well, that's nice, she said, sounding pleased and happy. That everybody's asking....

Me: Well, what's happened?

Lace: Oh, well, I can't tell you.

Me: You can tell me.

Lace: Oh, I can't....

Finally: I fell out of a tree, she said. I broke my arm.

It was true, too. She did. Break her arm. It was the left one, which, all things considered, was a good thing, since it wouldn't interfere quite so much with her art as if it had been her right one.

*

She broke her arm!!? Connor shouted the next morning in our design class, and then of course everybody knew.

Falling out of a tree?!!

Well, *that's* a new one....

Why?—that's what I want to know! *Why* was she up in a tree?

When she came back, she wouldn't tell us. She wouldn't talk about it at all.

Basically, I think Connor was sort of proud of her for having such an unusual accident. I know I was. I'm like Connor, I am a connoisseur and collector of Weird Stuff.

*

There was something that happened when you stayed out of school too much: you got a visit from Mr. Larson. Or: as we called him: just *Larson*.

You better watch it, Lace, the other students began to say: *Larson will come for you....*

You know how it is when you are in any school: even when you are older and ought to know better: something in you that is younger than your chronological age takes over; and you become afraid of things that would never in the world frighten you in your ordinary life.

So: Mr. Larson; *Larson*; a little mild-mannered man, with thinning hair and wire-rimmed glasses and a gentle way about him: a funny choice for Boogey Man, but there he was: our Boogey Man.

Lace was terrified of him.

Do you really think he'll come and find me? she said. Do you think he'll throw me out?

One day he came to talk to her in the cartooning class.

Cartooning was in a way fun and in another way boring after you had learned to do the right kind of drawing. Animation was what we worked on mostly, and animation was boring because you had to make the same damn drawing over and over on acetate sheets, and in each drawing a few things would change fractionally, so that when you put the drawings onto film and projected them the characters would appear to move.

At, say, five "frames"—-or drawings—a second, it would take for heaven's sake five drawings for a character to just *smile*.

(So from now on, dammit, I want you to appreciate those early Disney movies; they were not just works of art, they were also works of Herculean labor.)

Cartooning was incredibly tedious.

Mr. Larson's visit was a treat for most of us; it broke the monotony; but me and Connor were worried about Lace.

Con: Would they really kick her out?

Me: Maybe they'll put her on probation first....

Con: She's already been *warned*....

Me: They won't kick her out, Con...they want the tuition...they don't want to lose any of us....

Fingers crossed.

Larson took Lace over into a corner to talk to her. After a while we heard the two of them laughing like crazy, and—of all things!—Larson was moving his arms up and down, with his hands tucked into his armpits, like for heaven's sake those TV ads for Chicken Tonight, which is a kind of chicken-helper, along the lines of Hamburger-Helper, as far as I can make out. You have probably seen those ads.

And Lace was looking at him and drawing: her eyes were squeezed into slits in that funny squint artists have when they are trying hard to really *see* the thing in front of them.

What was *that* about, said Connor when Lace came back to our work space. I tried to listen, he said, but I couldn't hear much....

How rude, Con, said Lace: to try to listen.

Certainly, said Con. What else are ears for?

For heaven's sake, come to the point, I said: What did he say to you, Lace? Are you on probation?

Oh, Lace said, laughing, he was very nice. He was very kind. He said we could work something out....

I told him about my aunt dying...and Jerry's grandmother....
Really, he was *sweet*, she said.

For god's sake, said Connor. *Larson* was *sweet*?

And what was that arm-flapping business?

Oh, she said. And smiled. And laughed. I told him I was
having trouble with the duck in my animation drawings. I told
him I couldn't visualize how the wings would move up and down.
I mean, I can *see* the feet walking, but I can't *see* the wings.

So he was being a duck, she said.

Well. I just stared at her.

And Connor nearly had a stroke. He laughed so hard, huh-
huh-huh, that he actually fell off his work stool. Really and truly,
this did happen. Everyone stopped doing their acetate frames to
watch him flopping about on the floor.

He was being—a *duck*?—he screamed. Oh God—so funny—
Lace, you are *so funny*—

Oh, huh-huh-HUH! The flute laugh.

Why? said Lace, looking astonished at Connor's carryings-on.
What's the matter with *him*? she said. To me.

But I laughed at her too. Lace, you're too much, I said.
Larson comes in here to threaten you and before he leaves you
have him *imitating a duck*? You don't think that's funny?

Well, she said. Maybe a little.

Lace, I said, you're a natural resource. A national treasure.
You could charm birds out of trees. You should be on a protected
list, like the giraffe. People love you, Lace. You ought to be
bottled and sold. Or given away. Like holy water from Lourdes.

Oh, go on, she said. But she *was* pleased. She turned that
lovely pink color.

*

One day Lace was absent—for about the hundred and forty-
third time, practically—and when she came back and we asked her
why she was absent, she said she had attended the funeral of a
friend of her husband's who had committed suicide.

Connor was fascinated.

When? he said. How? He said.

Well, actually, Lace said, and her eyes were strange and far
away and the gray laughter was dimmed, actually he put his head
into a gas oven....

That really works, does it? said Connor. I've wondered.

Yes, said Lace.

Apparently, Con, I said. Since the man died....

You have to seal up the room, said Lace. To make it work really well.

What was his name, said Connor.

Marc, said Lace. Marcus....

Marcus, said Connor. Yes, okay....

A good enough name for a suicide, apparently.

Why did he do it, Lace? I said.

He was a Vietnam vet, Lace said. That's how Jerry met him, they were in a Vietnam vets organization together....

Her voice shook and tears stood in her eyes suddenly.

You don't have to talk about this, Lace, I said.

Was he married, said Connor.

Yes, Lace said. In fact, we both stayed with his wife last night, we slept over there...I am going back after school...Jerry is with her now...I only came today because I promised Mr. Larson....

This must be hard on Jerry, I said.

Fear leapt in Lace's eyes. Oh, yes, she said. Oh, yes.

*

I had no real sense at that time of Lace's husband, Jerry; and as a matter of fact, now that I know him, or at least have met him many times, I still don't have much of a notion of what he is like. Lace didn't talk about him much, and somehow the effect of what she did say was to make him shadowy, faceless. He was a veteran. He had been an addict and was trying to straighten himself out. He had been a biker and now drove a ramshackle truck that was always breaking down. During the warm months he worked in construction. He and Lace lived in a house in St. Paul that had been his family home. He went to a lot of funerals.

It wasn't enough.

But, you know, if Lace hadn't been right in front of me, she would have been shadowy and faceless too. Sometimes when she wasn't there, I couldn't remember what she looked like. Even now when I think of her, I think of gossamer, I think of the Cheshire Cat sitting in a tree, all smile, disappearing in front of your eyes.

*

Cat. Something happened about then that I think I need to put in here. I had a cat—named Littley, but that's another story—that I had put to sleep because she was sick so much of the time and had got to the point where she couldn't even walk up the stairs in my house by herself any more. If she wanted to go upstairs I had to carry her. And then I had to carry her down again. The animal was miserable, or so it seemed to me.

Also: this is the truth: Littley was a nuisance to me.

She cost me a lot of care and time, and a lot of money, which I did not have at that time, having no real job and going to school.

And if I were to tell the truth, I never liked that cat and she never liked me. She was really my daughter Margaret's cat, left with me when Margaret moved to Los Angeles.

So in a way I have to admit that it came as a relief when the cat got sick enough so that I felt justified in having her put down.

But I also felt awful guilt. Lord: I still do.

One night, soon after that, I was driving down Park Avenue on Minneapolis' south side, or Portland, whichever one is one-way going south, I never can remember, and a little cat that looked just like Littley ran right under the wheels of my car and I felt this awful little tiny *thump.*

I stopped the car by the curb and walked back about thirty feet. It was just a little thing and it was dead—in fact, I saw the life go out of it just as I came up to it and stooped down to touch it.

Have you ever seen the life go out of a creature? One second it is a living thing, breathing lungs, a beating heart, and the next second it is a scrap of fur.

Same thing with a human being. One second there and the next second: *gone.*

Oh where? Oh, where?

I thought: I have to find its owner. I went up and down knocking on doors—this was about 10:30 p.m. and Park Avenue (or Portland) is not exactly one of your better neighborhoods, I was pretty scared—and I could find no one who would claim ownership of the little cat.

Well, God. I had to give it up finally. I decided that the worst thing would be for some kid—the cat's owner?—to find it dead in the street, so I took it home and put it in a box—wrapped in a nice scarf of mine, poor kitty—and I buried it with appropriate prayers in my back yard, next to my guinea pig: Fred. Fred had a room of his own once: but that also is a whole other story. (That one actually has a title: *Fred's Room*.)

I expect you think this is crazy. I think so too.

I told Lace what I had done.

I thought she would see how crazy it was. I thought I would get some comfort from her for being such a dunce. I thought Lace could relate to all the duncery in the world.

But no: no comfort. No laughter: praise instead. Can you believe it?

She looked at me for a long time with those level, smiling gray eyes: and: That was a very nice thing you did, she said.

Maybe, I said. But crazy too, you have to admit it.

She ignored me.

Not very many people would have cared enough to have looked for the owner, she said. Not very many people would have taken the poor little thing home to bury it.....

Come on, Lace, I said. Anybody would have.

No, she said. Very few. You're a nice person, Joan, she said. She touched my hand, and you know, it's funny, but for a second there I felt beatified, blessed: I felt like a nice person. Wow: a positive epiphany.

*

Lace, I said to her once: well, actually, many times: what the hell were you doing up in that tree?

Finally she told me: I was rescuing a bird, she said. I was putting a baby bird back into its nest.

That was very nice of you, Lace, I said.

Don't they say you shouldn't do that, though? I said. Don't they say that the mother will never accept the baby after a human's hands have touched it?

They're wrong, she said.

*

We had a wonderful time at Vange's house the day we went to lunch.

Vange never does anything small, and we had this absolutely super lunch—well, dinner, really, you could have called it dinner, there was so much of it. A marvelous egg-plant casserole is the thing I remember mostly. And after we ate, Vange told fortunes with the gypsy cards.

Way back in her family tree somewhere, Vange claimed, there was a gypsy great- or great-great-grandmother, a Norwegian gypsy, honest to God, there really are Norwegian gypsies, and that ancestor read the gypsy cards. The skill was handed down through a lot of generations in the family, and now Vange had it.

She was really quite good, and not just at the cards, she could see things in a crystal ball too, and in tea leaves. At one time she read the tea leaves down at the Leaves Cafe in Minneapolis, do you remember it? It was quite a popular place a few years ago, maybe still is for all I know. You might have seen Vange there: younger then, of course; but even then fairly stout; with thick glasses and rolling-around eyes (nystagmus, she has) that see everything there is to see, and a lot of things that are not seen. Dark brown hair—iron gray now—cut fairly short and kept rather untidy; Vange has serious cowlicks, and even if she tried to keep her hair combed, it wouldn't work, the cowlicks would determine the style, or lack thereof. Never mind; it is the totality of Vange wherein the style inheres: Vange *is* a style.

Vange's given name is Evangeline Josephine, and she is named for two dead aunts.

Vange's house is like her: not a bit stylish, but after you get used to it you begin to come down off your high horse and you see that the house is completely original, that it has its own style. There is stuff all over, every surface is covered with stuff—and every piece of it means something, reminds Vange of something, some story, some person. Well: for example, that lamp is there in the dining room, the camel-skin lamp I told you about early on, the lamp in my dream. She had the lamp lit the day we were there: warm, soft light filtered through the vivid designs and turned the room dazzling.

Lots of other stuff: cups and vases, toys, a singing top I gave her for a Christmas long ago—we have been friends for many years now, Vange and I, twenty anyway—books and pictures, wall-hangings: everybody that ever made anything wanted to give one to Vange, and the whole house was like—well, yes, a rummage sale. A marvelous, marvelous rummage sale: better than the Vassar Sale.

It doesn't matter what you use, Vange says, meaning the cards or the leaves or the crystal ball. That's just a trick. She says. It only matters whether you have the gift.

Do me! Do me! clamored Connor after our lunch.

So Vange cleared off a space on the dining room table and read Connor's cards. She took out some of the cards—the twos, threes, and fours—and laid them aside, and then asked Connor to cut the rest of them—with his right hand and toward himself—into three piles. Then she laid them out in a pattern on the tablecloth. She used the large-print cards that are made especially for people who don't see well, and even so she bent down close to them to read them.

You're going to move, she said. I think within the next year. Far away to some warm place.

Oh! Connor said. Oh, I've been *thinking* and *thinking* of getting out of here! I've been thinking of going to Austin, Texas....

I see a house, Vange said. I see a big house down a residential street in a city, gray stone, not new, very substantial, a very nice house....

Maybe it's the fourth house, said Connor. He poked me. Giggled. Shut up, Con, I said. Pay attention.

I see a man, Vange said. He owns the house. He is gray-haired, I think; maybe blond, but I think gray. He is very good-looking, and he's rich.

She picked up the cards in a ritual order and laid them out in another pattern.

I see romance, she said: I think so.

With this older man? Connor said. Yes, I think so, said Vange.

Oh: Connor said. Oh, I have dreamed and dreamed of a man like that, an older man, rich and handsome, very *distingue*, very chic...who would love me...who would adore me....

His black eyes shone.

Well, I definitely see a man in the cards, said Vange.

Is it true love, Vange? said Connor. Will it last forever?

I don't see that far, said Vange: not to forever. I only see the man and the house.

And romance. Said Con.

And romance. Said Vange. Yes.

Oh, Vange! Connor said. You're a wonderful woman, I am *so* grateful to Joan for introducing us to you!

Vange laughed: her short, staccato laugh that can mean anything.

Thank you, she said. And smiled. Her plump face was like a Buddha's face: sees all, tells about half.

I like you and Lace too, she said. Very much. I think you are both delightful....

She went back to her perusal of the cards. Her hands sparkled over the cards, pointing, tapping, hovered and homed, like the hands had a sight independent of her eyes. The light from the camel-skin lamp cast vivid patterns on her hands and on the cards.

Hm, she said. Something else. I see something else in the cards.

You are very negative, Connor, she said. You tend to look for bad things, you expect the worst....

Don't do that any more, she said.

You are really a much better person than you think you are, Connor, she said. Much nicer.

Oh, no, he said: No, I am not nice. I am very haughty. I am very nasty and critical. I am temperamental. I am a vindictive little shit....

That's what you think you want to be, Connor, said Vange: What you really are is quite different from what you think you are....

She turned to me: would you agree with me, Joan? she said.

Oh, absolutely, I said.

I've told you, Connor, I said. You are kind, you are a kind person, you have great kindness....

Oh, I *am not*, said Connor. I *do not*. I am a ruthless bastard, he said.

Have it your own way, Con, I said. And we all laughed at him.

*

What about you, Lace? said Connor. Let Vange do your fortune now. Fear flashed in Lace's eyes. She stiffened and pulled away, wrapped her arms around herself and shivered.

Oh, no, she said: Oh no not me....

I couldn't....

But why, Lace, said Connor.

It's so much fun, Vange is so good....

Oh, I'd be too afraid, said Lace.

I don't want to know the future, she said.

*

One morning: in our design class: I dreamed about your fourth house, Joan, Connor said.

I stared at him. You're making that up, Connor, I said.

No, honestly, he said. We were all there in the dream, you and me and Lace, and the fourth house was *Love. Amour. True love forever*.

He rolled his eyes and batted his lashes at me. Honestly, Con: I said. You'd make fun of anything.

There was a perfectly marvy man there, an older man, who took me just as I am, and adored me....

Unconditional love, I said. What the therapists talk about.

Oh, *yes*, said Con. His face was shining like a thin dark sun. Connor laughed all the time, at anything, but he really did believe in things, you know. Dreams coming true. And like that.

Well, good luck to you, I said. Old Grumpy here. Talk about Connor being negative.

Maybe the dream was a prophecy, he said.

Maybe, I said.

Vange said I'd find him, he said.

I seem to recall that she said something like that, I said.

She said I'd find him, Connor said.

*

Why did I stay with them? I could have gone with any of the others. Leandra, for example. Well, I stayed for lots of reasons. But mainly I think it was that I loved them both. Connor didn't know it, but he already had his unconditional love—but from someone—me—who didn't count. Isn't that the way, though? That it goes?

*

What do you think, Lace? said Connor. For a wonder, Lace was there on time for the 8:30 class. I think the interview with

29

Larson had had its effect: I think she became ashamed to make life difficult for such a nice man.

I think the fourth house is Suffering, Lace said; and bent over her drawing.

*

The Rockettes were coming to town from Radio City in New York, and Connor was all excited about this. He ran around like a little black-eyed bird getting ready for it.

The *Rockettes!* he chirped. They are *so good!* They are *so wonderful!* That incredible *precision!*

Blah, blah. On and on.

Anyway, they were going to be in a parade down Nicollet Mall, and we all went to see them, the whole class, I mean. Connor took his camera along. Lace too.

Not me. What did I care about the Rockettes? So silly. Jesus, even the *name*. I mean. For heaven's sake.

So we were strolling along the mall where the parade was supposed to be coming along, any time now, hurrying really, Connor made us hurry, he was so anxious and eager: What If We Miss Them, I'll Kill Myself; honestly, Con; and suddenly Connor was gone.

He was walking along with us and he disappeared. Just like that. One second he was there and the next second he wasn't.

Where's Connor? I said to Lace.

We looked and looked. No Con. Not anywhere. Finally we gave up and just enjoyed the crowd and the parade. Lace took a few pictures.

We never did find Con that afternoon, but the next day he told us that he had heard music in the distance and ran off to find it. Eventually he had climbed up a street-lamp pole with his camera and filmed the Rockettes from that height.

People thought I was a real news photographer, he said. They gave me a boost up the pole. He laughed, enchanted with the memory.

God. He was so pleased with himself that day.

And actually he did get some decent shots.

*

About the middle of our second year at MTI Connor moved into a new apartment. He had been complaining about the old one for a long time—really ever since poor old discarded Stanton had cleaned it, which was more than a year before.

Actually, it's not an apartment, he told us. It's a *space*. It's an *art space*.

Is it a loft, Con? Lace said.

Well—not exactly, he said. I couldn't find a loft that suited me. But the rooms are *huge*—like a loft—and the light is magnificent....

He was on and on about the light and the space.

I'm painting it *all white*, he said.

So stark. His eyes sparkled black.

Well, anyway, finally the apartment was ready: I'm moving in on Saturday, he said.

Have you got enough help for moving, Con? I said. I mean, I did have a car at home in my garage, and I could drive if I needed to.

Oh, yes, he said: My friends from La Tortue are helping me.

His other life.

One day he invited us to come and see the new place. Well. He invited me, and I invited Lace.

Lace didn't want to go.

She had one excuse and then another.

Finally: Please, Lace, I said. I honestly think we should. I think Connor needs us to come. Truly I do.

Lace was skeptical. Oh, I don't think he cares that much, she said. About my opinion. Yours maybe.

I think he does, I said: I think we represent the world or something. The world outside of La Tortue, maybe. I don't think he has any other friends. Do you?

Well, anyway, friends or not, I finally talked her into it and we went to pay a call on Connor in his space.

The apartment—certainly it was an apartment—was nice. Elegant—an old building with beautiful molding and floors and cabinets. It overlooked Loring Park, second floor as I recall, and the white walls with the big windows, lots of windows, were very effective.

Nice, Con, I said.

Nice, said Lace.

But look at the *rug*, Con said. Look at the *sofa*. Look at the *chaise*.

The rug was gorgeous. Room-size, maybe 9x12, some kind of Persian. Wonderful colors—you could lose yourself in them; like a kaleidoscope, like a dream of Paradise.

It's like your dream, Joan, said Lace: the big rummage sale....

The sofa was an *empire* antique. Looked to be, anyway. Ditto the *chaise longue*.

My God, Con, I said. Where did you *find* them? Where did you *get* them?

I bought them, said Con. From that antique place on Lagoon.

Bought them, I said. But are they *real?* I said: I can't believe they're *real*....

They're real, said Con. Of course they're real. You don't think I'd have something that wasn't real, do you?

But weren't they terribly expensive, Con? I said.

Terribly, he said. Yes.

Lace was absolutely silent. Me too, finally.

Dumbstruck, actually. Yes. You could say we were.

Connor was simply delighted at our reaction. Eliciting enthusiasm is one thing, but striking folks dumb is a whole higher level, isn't it?

Here's my studio, Con said, and ushered us into a big, light room with an art table and an awesome array of art supplies: there seemed to be every known variety of brush, pencils, pens, every kind we'd ever worked with and many I didn't know about.

Tons of paper. Well, anyway, lots.

Will you look at the *paper*, I said.

Arches, he said.

(For your information, reader, *Arches* was then, maybe still is, the *creme de la creme* of paper.)

What else, I said.

Would you like some refreshment? said Con.

Refreshment: wow.

Sure, I said. No, said Lace.

We have to go, said Lace.

Ten minutes, Lace, I said. Quarter of an hour.

So we stayed, and Con served a gourmet coffee with some odd but quite good flavoring and—what's that Middle Eastern dessert? made with honey? *harissa*? Something like that.

Delicious.

Then: I really have to go, said Lace. Jerry expects me at home.

So we went then.

Can I give you a ride home, Joan? Lace said, as we crossed over the street back to the school.

Do you have time to do that? I said.

Oh, yes, sure, she said.

We went to the school's parking garage across Hennepin and found Jerry's truck: a big old rusted-out red truck. I had considerable difficulty hoisting myself into the cab, it was so high off the ground.

Do you need any help? said Lace.

I can manage, I said. And pulled myself up. And into.

You know what they say, Lace: "That first step is a bitch." I said.

She laughed.

Yeah, she said.

She stopped the truck in front of my house on Bryant Avenue in South Minneapolis.

Come in? I said.

No, she said. Not today. I don't think so.

One place a day is enough, she said.

What does that mean, Lace? I said.

Oh, well...when you see where people live, they begin to be real to you, Lace said. Then you have to start worrying about them.

*

I wondered how on earth Connor got that much money—could the tips at La Tortue have been that good? I never had the guts to ask him though.

*

I see Lace every now and then, maybe once a year, maybe even less than that, since we graduated from the art program. She has had many jobs since, but has done well at none of them, and has liked none of them. None of her jobs was as an artist.

Connor I've lost track of completely.

I know that he went to Austin, and that he did meet a man there.

The last news I had of him was written on a Christmas card. The card shows an exquisite clown jugging the moon and the stars. I liked the card so much that I put it into a frame and hung it on my dining room wall.

So whatever the last news was is now inaccessible, folded inside the framed card: written in Con's mannered, loopy handwriting. Oh, I guess I could unframe it and read it, but what would be the point?—Connor is lost to me. To us.

Letters sent to the last address I have for him come back marked: *Addressee Unknown.*

Maybe he's dead, Lace says: I think he'd write to us if he was alive. Her voice is sad, but nevertheless there is still laughter in it.

Maybe he died of AIDS.

Maybe, I say. It certainly could have happened: I say: he was such a fickle little guy, looking all over for his marvy older man, swishing that cute little ass of his around....

Joan! Lace says. She turns pink, like a valentine: blond hair curls around her face like a ruffled edging.

But it *was* cute, she says: wasn't it? She laughs.

Other times I think that he might have killed himself, she says; he was so interested when Marcus died.

Wanting to know how he did it and all. She says. The laughter in her eyes is haunted by many, many ghosts: the dead, the dying.

Us. Poor old Lace, carrying all of us around, worrying about all of us.

I care about Connor, she says.

I know you do, Lace, I say.

And in her eyes I see Connor walking down the corridor of his life, gesturing and posing and laughing, twin Connors, one in each of Lace's eyes, never to meet in this world.

*

There are days when it pleases me to think that the fourth house is the house of heart's desire, where marvy older men are counted in the dozens, and little cats never get killed in the street, and talent goes to the people who really need it. Nobody ever gets fired—well, more, nobody is born blind. Everybody is fast as lightning. Everybody likes their haircuts. There are no protected lists, because everything is protected, and there isn't any K.I.; and the title "Ordinary People" can be used again and again, because ordinary people are considered to be so valuable. Mothers and daughters are in every case a perfect match.

Everybody goes to MCAD. Or Harvard.

Yale.

Whatever.

Lord have...mercy...on such...as we....

SUNSIGHT

Sunsight was a New Age bookstore in Minneapolis many years ago, maybe thirty years ago or more. Minneapolis was at that time considered by occultists—there was some reason for the idea of "occult" in those days: occult means hidden, secret; and occultists in those days believed that they did have something secret: but nowadays all the secrets are told, all the cats are out of the bag, the "occult" is pretty much main-stream, a president consults an astrologer—anyway (back to my original sentence here) Minneapolis was considered by occultists to be located exactly at a crossroads of some vibrational something-or-other; and the hub of the occult universe.

Sunsight-the-bookstore was by this theory also at the hub of the universe. The vibrational whatever.

The owner, Shari Duvalle, otherwise known as Morning, a name that was given to her in a séance or a trance or something, was certainly convinced that *she* was at the hub of the universe.

Shari (Morning) was a pleasant, pretty, plump woman, maybe thirty or thirty-five, maybe even forty; she was getting interested in menopause—wanted me to find someone who could teach a class in holistic menopause—so maybe she was forty or more, but she looked and seemed very young. Fluffy brown hair, serene brown eyes, white flawless skin, and an air of being above-it-all and considerably better-than.

Shari looked thoroughly mainstream—dressed for success, etc. But what came out of her mouth was—even for that time— pretty off-the-wall. (Hey—now we talk about the world turning over on its axis in 2012....)

Shari's consort—she may have been married to him, but I was never sure of this—was a guy named Richard: Rick, they called him. Rick seemed a lot older than Shari, and a lot more worldly.

Shari seemed—most of the time—unworldly or other-worldly, but Rick seemed to make it with a foot in both worlds. At least that appeared to be his intention.

(I don't trust anybody who claims to be spiritual, he said once.)

Rick had a black goatee, hooded black eyes, and a slight accent that was said to be French-Canadian. You know that accent. Celine Dion has it. For example.

There were a few other people working at Sunsight too at the time I came: Denise, who handled all the inventory and book-keeping; Jaime, a young woman who was a part-time clerk; and Wally, who swept up and did odd jobs.

Actually, though, everybody there waited on customers, and everybody was available to sweep up and dust and so on. Nobody except Denise had a defined job.

Well, and me. I had a job. I was hired out of art school—Minneapolis Technical Institute, where I took a two-year sequence in commercial art after I quit my social work job—I was hired as the editor of the store's monthly publication, called—what else?—*Sunsightings.*

The publication had a logo of a rising sun that I personally hated, but was stuck with, because Shari and Rick had just paid a heap of money for someone to design it for them. And there wasn't a lot of money to spare. That became clear almost right away. The store was operating more or less hand-to-mouth.

There were a bunch of outside folks, experts in one thing and another, connected with the store: Augusta, who took folks on Spiritual Journeys; Ben, who was a numerologist; Kathleen, an astrologer; a witch (white, of course) etc., etc.: and these outside folks taught classes in some basement rooms under the bookstore. Underneath the basement was a sub-basement. I never went there. Supplies were kept there, I understood.

Part of my job as editor of the newsletter was to coordinate the teachers and classes. Make sure that two of them didn't get assigned to the same room at the same time. For example. Arrange it so that two people who hated each other wouldn't be scheduled on the same night. Like that.

And, hey. These people were temperamental and jealous as hell: these other-worldly folk. One time somebody walked into a room where Augusta was getting ready for a class, and she was mad as hell. She said she was half-ascended, and now would have to come out of it and clean up the room's vibrations all over again.

Half-ascended? I said.

Is that anything like half in the bag?

Well: not funny, guys.

If looks could kill, I'd be dead now.

This is an awful lot of explanation, isn't it? Kind of boring for you? But hey, you have to get the whole picture, or else this story won't make any sense. Maybe it won't make any sense anyway. Maybe it isn't meant to.

You know: like, *meant?*

I don't know how I heard about the job. Maybe it was posted at Amazon Books; I used to drop in there occasionally. Anyway, hear about it I did. And—just out of art school, metamorphosing (is that a word?) from a social worker into a, what? free spirit? intending to change from a drone into a butterfly (Hey, I'm aware that it doesn't work that way, but you know what I mean)—I applied for the job. I walked in with my terrific portfolio of wonderful art: hey, I thought so, and my teachers thought so too: and I applied.

They gave me an interview.

We sat in a back room—office?—on a couple of those weird slingshot chairs and a floor cushion, me and Shari and Rick.

Shari, in a very smart black pants-suit, started out sitting in one of the chairs, and Rick was on the cushion, but before we got underway Shari decided that the arrangement was not to her liking and she changed places with Rick, sat cross-legged on the cushion in her nice suit.

Do you have a resume, said Rick, settling into his new chair, looking pretty uncomfortable. It is not easy to conduct business from the laid-back posture that a slingshot chair demands.

I handed him my resume.

I don't have a lot of experience, I said. Not in this area. As a social worker I have a great resume. But I'm not a social worker any more. I'm an artist and a writer. I'm changing, I'm metamorphosing....

I thought that would get them, that metamorphosis bit.

But: That's nice, said Shari.

Whoops.

Make a note: metamorphosis is *out.*

Do you know much about what we are trying to do here at Sunsight?

Said Rick.

Uh—not much: I said. Some.

We couldn't pay a lot, he said.

Shari-Morning waved her hand in a floating, flowing gesture, like a little queen.

She's right for it, Richard, she said.

Hey! Folks! I was *right* for it!

She hasn't got any experience, said Rick. She doesn't know anything about our business....

She can learn. Said Shari. Can't you, Joan?

Joan, that was me.

Her name is right too, she said. Joan. John. Jehovah. "God has been gracious."

Shari/Morning was into names at that period, I learned later. She was trying to get people to change their names, as she had changed hers.

But my name, it seemed, was okay. I mean, Jeez: "God has been gracious." You don't get a whole lot better than that.

Shari reached out her little white plump paw and took my hand.

Can't you, dear?

Learn?

She said.

I can learn, I said. More or less mesmerized. I never altogether fell under the Morning spell, but I had to admit that there *was*...something...about her....

But, said Rick.

I want her, Richard, said Shari. I believe she has been sent.

Rick was clearly under the spell; but he was at the same time a little exasperated. He grimaced, but: Okay, Shari, he said. It's your call.

Call me Morning, Richard, she said. Please. Smiled at him: wow. Six hundred watts.

Okay, said Rick. Okay, Morning. Smiled. Smirked.

Oh, he was under the spell, all right. But there was something else going on there too. Something else looked out of the hooded flat black eyes.

*

The other day I was talking to my brother David on the phone—yeah, we are fogies, we don't *text*, we actually *talk*. Hear one another's voices.

I don't recall how we got onto it, or what the original subject was. But: Well, hell, why does it matter, Dave said. The world is going to end in 2012 anyway.

Or so some people say.

Laughed. Ha-ha.

No, no, Dave, I said.

You've got it wrong.

Some people think 2012 will be the end, Armageddon, the end of the Mayan calendar, like that. But *other* people, just as many, think it will be a new beginning. The whole world will, like, turn over on its axis, and everything will change. Everything will tip over. People's psychological wiring will change: people *are* electric, you know, they have electricity in them.

Well, yeah, said Dave the—formerly—big-shot engineer. That's true: that people have electricity in their bodies. But what good will it do them to tip over?

I don't know how it will work, Dave, I said. But people's hearts will change.

They will suddenly see how it is possible to live on this earth in peace. They will see differently out of their eyes.

That's what some people say. That's what I choose to believe.

I don't know, said Dave. I kind of prefer the Armageddon idea.

If I have to choose one.

*

And that's how I came to work at Sunsight. Because Morning wanted me, experience or no. Because I had been sent.

Four-fifty an hour, said Rick.

Sorry. I won't work for less than five. Said I. (That's what they told us at the school. Minimum five. No trained artist should work for less than five dollars an hour. They said. Obviously this was a while ago. Nowadays, McDonald's can't hire for five dollars an hour.)

Four-fifty for a training period, Shari said. Morning said. One month. Then five dollars, if it works out.

Okay, I said.

Hey, it *would* work out. Hadn't I been *sent?*

*

Yeah, but for *what?* The ways of the Lord are mysterious. Any lord.

You know what Spenser says: *The ways of the Lord are mysterious, but seldom pleasant.*

That's Spenser the detective, not Spenser the poet. My literary allusions are kind of lowbrow. As am I.

*

Denise was very nice. She was attractive, in a sort of gaunt and bony way, and was very aware of herself. If you know what I mean. She was always trying on earrings from stock, looking at them in a little mirror at the counter. When there were no customers to see her.

She was always admiring her fingers with new rings on them, as the rings came in. Her long painted fingernails were flawless.

Are you surprised that there were earrings and rings in a bookstore? Hey, yeah, there were all sorts of things besides books, more and more coming every day, crystal balls and marble unicorns, masks, bells, candles. Etc., etc. *Bell, book and candle.* All over the place. Crowded onto shelves and into locked glass cabinets: locked because some of the stuff was pretty valuable. I mean, like $75 for some of the feather masks. For example. $75 was a tremendous lot of money then.

That's why we're always short of money, Denise told me one day, *sotto voce.* When nobody was around. *Sotto voce* anyway: whether people were around or not: *sotto voce* was Denise's style. I was grateful for Denise: nobody else told me anything. Everybody else seemed to think that I should *just know.*

Just Knowing can be difficult.

We're stock-poor, said Denise.

It's Shari.

She can't resist pretty things.

Well, but I can relate to that. Said Denise. Batting her clearly false eyelashes at a ring on her finger. Moving her hand so that facets of the ring's green stone caught the light from the windows and flashed and sparkled.

Your fingernails are beautiful, Denise, I said. How do you get them that way? So long, but, you know, not curving under, the way most people's do when they get long?

They're fake, said Denise.

I wouldn't have guessed. I said.

There's a lot of stuff going on here that you wouldn't guess. Said Denise.

And: smirking: I try to think that I bring a little sunshine into every day. She said. Waving the fake fingernails. Smirking again. Eyebrows rising.

Anyway, she said, Shari buys way too much stuff.

I thought you were in charge of inventory, I said.

After it comes in, said Denise.

Nobody buys except Shari.

But hey, why not? It's her store.

She said.

Not Rick's? I said.

Oh, no, said Denise. Batting the eyelashes again. Wiggling her ringed fingers. Knowing she was funny. Self-conscious.

Not Rick's. She said. No way. No fucking way.

*

Reading this story over, I can see that up to here the tone is pretty snotty. Like I thought all this occult stuff was garbage. Another Opiate of the People—like that. Like I was above it.

I don't really mean it that way. I think some of it was garbage and some of it was a clear stream of knowledge from the other side.

Other Side? I can hear you saying it,

Yeah, other side. Schopenhauer believed in it. Why can't you? I? You know what S. wrote: something like this: *On the other side of the veil that we call death there is a light compared to which our sun is but a shadow.*

Well, wow.

Einstein believed in it. Or something like it. And Einstein was The Man of the last Century. So said Time Magazine in the Millennium issue, anyway.

You don't have to call it God. If that's the sticking point. You can call it anything.

You can do it, babe. For the time it takes to read this story, anyway. You can have what they call a temporary suspension of disbelief.

Let's cut these people a little slack, you and I both—okay? No more snotty put-downs. I promise. Hard as it is for me. I mean, I am a snotty-put-down kind of *person*.

Can I help doing it?—well, we'll see, won't we?

At that time, my personal life was going to hell in a hand basket. I was sharing an apartment with a friend: I had this idea that I was getting too old to cut the grass at my house and do other work like that: for God's sake, I was only about fifty-two; now I am seventy-six, and every time I cut the grass in my yard I thank God that I have grass to cut; anyway, I rented out my house and moved into an apartment with this friend to see if I'd like apartment living, and folks, I *didn't* like it, I *hated* it.

And I was stuck with a year's lease. Being cheaper than lentils, cheaper than Jack Benny—if you remember Jack Benny, you are pretty old, as old as me—I couldn't make up my mind to just pay the money on the lease, take the loss and chalk it up to, as they say, experience. So I stayed in that apartment and hated my whole life.

My plants were dying.

My relationship was breaking up.

My mental state was something along the lines of suicidal.

I could not see any light at all at the end of any tunnel.

So the job at Sunsight came along as a form of rescue. For eight hours a day or so, I was rescued from my life.

I should kiss those people's feet instead of making fun of them.

*

Wally, the kid who swept up, in the store and out on the sidewalk—well, actually, he was a man, I mean if it is not p.c. to call a female person over the age of twelve a girl, I guess I can't call Wally a *kid*—Wally, the *young man* who swept up and carried boxes and what-have-you, was probably somewhat retarded or maybe mentally ill. Autistic. Or something. Nobody ever said so, it was one of the things you had to Just Know.

He was kind of sweet, Wally, very obliging, very accommodating: fetching things for people, lifting down high-up stuff if you asked him to, like that. He was tall, lanky, moved slowly. His tow-hair had a turquoise streak in it. Morning/Shari renewed the streak every couple of weeks.

Wally loved the masks in the store: feather masks, porcelain masks, papier mache.

Sometimes I would see him leaning on his broom, just staring at one of the feather masks in its glass cabinet: one mask in particular that he seemed fascinated by. That mask was so expensive that no one had ever bought it, least of all Wally, who probably made less money than I did. Chances were pretty good that no one ever would buy it. So in effect, Wally as good as owned the mask.

Wally didn't talk much. I mean, he wasn't mute or anything, he *could* talk, but he didn't. Much. Denise told me that he had named his mask, but she couldn't remember what the name was.

I hear you've named the mask, I said to him one day when I found him standing and staring at it.

Silence.

What's its name? I said.

He turned dark red—a blush to end all blushes. But: Ka-blub-blub, he said.

Something like that. .

What is it that you like about it? I said. That one in particular?

Well: Mutter, mutter.

But I persisted. What? I said. Please tell me, Wally, I am really interested.

He has no eyes, he managed at last. His eyes are lost. But he knows things.

He sees things out of his lost eyes.

*

Wally loved Denise. He did her bidding like he was her slave. And then asked for more tasks.

Well, she was kind to him: that was it.

What's the matter with Wally? I said to her. With his head? Is he retarded?

Nothing's wrong, she said. Laughed.

But then: Well, I admit that he's not just like the rest of us.

But that's not exactly a liability.

Is it?

Said Denise.

I guess not, I said.

No, he's not retarded, she said. Actually he's very smart. He likes you. For example.

That's smart. I said.

We both laughed—one of those sweet moments that come now and then when angels look out of our mortal eyes and salute one another.

Hey, who's crazy now?

*

Sometimes Denise let Wally help stock the shelves—as a sort of special treat, I think. One day: Hey, he said—to Denise— where should this go?

He was holding a crystal ball, maybe four inches in diameter.

Over here, Denise said. By the rest of the crystal stuff.

And look in the box some more. It should have a little stand, a holder of some kind.

Wally unwrapped more stuff.

Here it is, he said.

Oh, Dennis, he said. It's little gold horses! Little gold horses to hold up the ball!

Denise looked at Wally with sudden sharpness in her eyes. Wally caught the look and flushed that awful dark red color again.

Denise, he said.

They're unicorns, said Denise. Not horses.

Unicorns? said Wally.

A unicorn is a wonderful and rare animal, Denise said.

You are a unicorn, Wally, she said. In a manner of speaking. *Dennis?*

*

After I had been at Sunsight for a month, and after I'd produced one newsletter, Rick and I sat down together in the "office", and he told me that I'd passed the test and would thereafter be considered a permanent employee.

At five dollars an hour? I said.

We can't afford five, he said. Sorry.

Shari said you'd raise me to five dollars an hour after a trial period.

Oh, he said. Um. Did she really say that?

Hey, you heard her. Jerk. What are you trying to pull here?

She did, I said.

And: I can't stay for less than five.

Oh well then, he said. I guess. If Shari said so.

Grumpily.

It's not going to matter anyway, he said. Soon. The store will go under. Soon.

Lord, I said: alarmed: for myself. Is it that bad?

Well, no, said Rick. Not exactly. Laughed.

Shari—Morning—says I'm too pessimistic. He said. Too negative. She says the Universe will provide. She's burning the money-candle at this very moment. Even as we speak.

Rick's black eyes were flat, but I thought I saw a funny glint in them for a second.

Zing!—that fast.

Laughter?

Did he believe? I never found out. I never knew.

Maybe he believed in Shari: Morning. Sort of. In a way. Hey. As much as I did. But I wasn't her consort, was I? I didn't need to believe. I just needed to take home the money. Five dollars an hour.

Of course, it's a lot more fun if you believe.

*

One day I was wandering around in the basement, making a chart of the rooms and who was going to teach in them, and when, and what.

There were three rooms, one large and two small, and a whole lot of people to schedule into them. And since a lot of those people hated one another's guts, it was not an easy task.

There *is* no white witchcraft in the Twin Cities, Ben, the numerologist, said. It's all black. Every bit of it. *I know this.*

Numerology is superstitious crap, said Augusta, the soul-travel conductor.

This is just to give you an example of how they felt about each other. This is to show you how problematic the scheduling was.

Scheduling—anything—is easy if you leave out the human factor, but as soon as you put it in—well, wow. Human=difficult. I guess you know this.

*

There was a door at the end of the hall in the basement, beyond the smallest room.

What does that door lead to? I said to Denise.

Who happened to be in the basement with me that day. Doing God knows what. The Universe knows what. There I go again. I can't seem to be anything but snotty, can I? I warned you. I told you that I was a snotty-put-down kind of person.

Can I change? Oh, I hope so. I think so. Maybe.

That's the door to the sub-basement, she said. You don't ever need to go down there. You wouldn't like it. It's dirty. It's damp. This building is really old. The foundations are crumbling, a bit. There are spiders. Maybe there are rats. Rick says there are rats down there.

She shivered.

I wouldn't go down there, she said. Not on a bet.

*

Well. But I wanted to see for myself, didn't I? Curious Georgia opened the sub-basement door and carefully propped it open with a handy brick, so as not to cut off the light.

Went down a flight of rickety wooden stairs.

Dirty, oh, yeah.

The dirt of a century, at least, was down there. Overhead, out in the middle of the room, hanging from the ceiling, was a bare light bulb with a string attached. For turning the light on, I guessed. I reached for the string. But it dangled just above my fingers. I jumped at it a couple of times, but there was no way. Apparently only tall people used that basement. Well. Only Rick, probably. I don't think they could have got Wally down there if they'd tied him up first.

Oh, well.

By the light from the door, I could see old furniture piled against all four walls. Boxes. Crates. One table, cleaned up some, held new-looking corrugated cardboard boxes.

White Wave, the boxes said.

I opened one. Toilet paper. Hey, sure, you have to keep it somewhere, don't you?

There was another door at the end of the room. I went through it. Again, old furniture piled up. An ancient furnace. Ducts. Another room opened off this one.

Why. The place was a rabbit warren.

I went as far as I could see to go.

Suddenly the light was cut off and I was in pitch-darkness.

I stood stock-still and tried to collect myself.

Go back to the door.

Obviously. It must have closed by accident. Maybe someone saw it and figured everybody else was gone: it was almost quitting time for most people.

I would be okay. I would be fine. In my mind I pictured the layout of the room I had just come through. I groped my way back, crashing into anonymous junk. Again and again. Found a wall, groped along it. Found a doorway.

I finally reached—in the dark—the room I'd first come into, with the wooden stairs leading up. Oh, relief.

But there was no light, not even a crack. It must have been a very tight door. It must have slammed shut. But how could it? I left it propped. I climbed up the stairs. Well. Crawled up, actually. Getting dirty? Hey, who was counting?

The door was locked.

I pounded on it.

No answer. Nothing.

Began to yell.

Hey! Somebody! Let me out! Open the goddamn door!

Well. Nothing. Nobody.

I sat on those crazy stairs pounding and screaming for what seemed like an hour. My hands hurt, I pounded so hard.

No answer. Nobody came.

No one would ever find me. I knew this. I would, like, *die* down here in the dark.

I was very scared.

I heard strange scrabbling noises.

Rats?

Denise said there were rats.

Oh, God. Oh, God, help me.

Yes, I actually turned to prayer. *There are no atheists, etc....*

After a while I saw that the darkness was not total. I could begin to see faint outlines of objects, black against black. Maybe my eyes were accommodating. That happens, you know. If there is even one little crack of light. I know this from reading about spelunkers: cave people.

Sanity: some: set in. My brain, my big, over-developed human brain started to work. Where, I thought, is the light coming from? It has to be coming from somewhere....

I left my perch on the stairs and began to grope my way—the darkness was still pretty deep, too deep to just stride along— through the rooms I'd been in before, and then beyond them. The little hint of light got stronger.

Finally I saw the source. It was a grate high above my head, maybe fifteen feet above. Sunlight was streaming down through it and making a pattern on the floor. My God, I thought. I'm under the sidewalk. I'm under the street.

Suddenly motes of dust fell down and dappled the sun shaft. And a sound: swish, swish.

A broom.

Wally, I whispered. Is that you?

Wally, I yelled.

The sweeping stopped.

Wally! Down here! *Under the grate!*

Wally's face, astounded, appeared, stripes of face between the iron bars of the grate.

Is it somebody? his voice quavered. Is it a person?

Certainly it's a person! I yelled. It's me! Joan!

Old "God is Gracious," I thought. Still snotty, see?

The One Who Was Sent.

For what? For what?

Joan? Wally said.

Yeah, I said.

What are you doing down there, Joan?

Oh, right. First things first.

Let me out, I said. For God's sake.

How should I do that, Joan? he said. His fingers curled around the grate's bars and he pulled.

Uh, uh, uh....

Can't do it, Joan...it's stuck....

Go to the door in the basement, Wally, I said. Open it. I'll meet you back there....

*

Well, anyway, I got out. A dirty and scraped and banged-up mess. I never found out who had shut and locked the door. No one ever admitted it. Maybe it was Rick, who, as it turned out, had left early with Morning that day.

Maybe it was Morning.

*

I *told* you not to go down there, said Denise. I did tell you....

Hey, were there rats? she said.

Practically rubbing her hands together, hoping.

There were rats, I said. I think so.

It's absolutely amazing how one person's disaster is another person's entertainment. Even Denise. Nice Denise.

Her wonderful red fingernails—fake—waved in the air. Her graceful hands floated. Her rings winked and sparkled.

Were you scared? she said.

Shitless, I said.

Were you scared, Joan? said Wally.

Yes, Wally, I was very scared, I said.

He took my hand in his and patted it.

Sometimes I get scared, he said. I know how it is, Joan.

I think it's a miracle that I was out there, Joan, he said, after we all got up the stairs and back into the store. I mean, what if I hadn't swept out there today?

Wally, you always sweep the sidewalk at the end of the day, said Denise.

It was a miracle, said Wally.

Okay, it was a miracle, said Denise.

Ka-blub-blub did it, Wally said.

How's that work? said Denise.

I was talking to him, said Wally. Just before I decided to go out and sweep. I think he saw Joan with his lost eyes and told me to do that.

You didn't *decide* to sweep, Denise said. You *always* sweep. It's your job.

I think it was a miracle, Wally said.

From *my* point of view, if anybody cares about that, I said, from *my* point of view it was definitely a miracle.

Seeing the sun shine through that grate, that was a miracle too. It felt like a miracle.

Both of you, said Denise, are nuts.

It just happened. That's all.

Said Denise.

No, said Wally. It was a miracle, wasn't it, Joan?

It was a miracle, Wally, I said.

Done through you.

And Ka-blub-blub. Said Wally.

Right. And Ka-blub-blub.

Denise said I was a rare and wonderful animal, didn't she, Joan? Said Wally.

Right, Wally, I said. She did. And so you are: rare and wonderful.

*

I sat in a tatty velvet-covered chair by the counter and they both hovered over me.

Are you all right now, Joan? said Denise.

I'm all right, I said.

Now.

Then we'd better lock up. Said Denise. It's time. Past time.

So we all three gathered our belongings together and left by the front door, and Denise locked the door.

Another day, another dollar, she said. To coin a phrase.

Come on, Denise. You believe in miracles. I know you do. Said I.

Well, you got me, said Denise. Yeah. I believe. I'm just too crabby to admit it in public.

We got her, Joan! gloated Wally. We got her....

And so the three of us, believers all, Crabby, Snotty, and the Unicorn, went our separate ways down the street. I went to the bus stop on the corner. Wally unlocked a bike from the store's bike rack and pedaled off. Denise turned East on Lake Street and walked away.

*

Sunsight did close its doors forever not long after that: not more than a couple of years later. Apparently a money-candle will take you only just so far. But it served its purpose for me—it seems to me that I have been following a faint glimmer of light ever since, a faint, beckoning sight of sun.

And I finally got whatever it took—common sense, surrendering cheapness, whatever—paid up my lease and went back into my house, where I most happily cut the grass.

A miracle? Hey, maybe.

And maybe 2012 will produce another miracle, a change in our human hearts. Maybe our lost eyes will at last see a metamorphosis.

I'm going to believe it anyway. I'm going to choose to believe.

Like I said before, it's more fun that way.

LABYRINTH

I

I had two wedding days with the same guy. God knows the first wedding day was bad enough, with my mother threatening to jump off a bridge, and the groom—I should have figured something out from this, right?—two hours late and broke, having to borrow from me the money for flowers.

And he wouldn't wear a ring—said he saw a ring as a symbol of bondage.

Before the wedding, I was in New York visiting a dear friend, Elinor, who had been my freshman English teacher at the University of Minnesota, when I got—long distance and by letter—engaged.

I think, wrote Bud, when he heard that I was going out with other guys in NYC, *I think we should consider ourselves engaged.*

Engaged! said Elinor. My little girl! Engaged!

And: Is he going to give you a ring?

Uh—I don't think so, I said.

Why not?

He doesn't believe in rings.

We don't believe in rings.

We see rings as symbols of bondage.

We. Get that *we.* I am an Aries: my sun sign is Aries. Aries people are loyal to the point of lunacy.

*

Even my father—when I got back home to Minneapolis—said I had to have an engagement ring.

Give her yours, Elizabeth, he said to my mother. She'll get it when you die anyway.

Holy mackerel! Callous? You bet. I may have had a small glimmer of it then, but now I feel major guilt. I shouldn't have let him do it. I know that now. But then, I only felt—Oh, boy, I'll have a diamond ring! Like everybody else!

She took it off her finger and gave it to me. I remember it like it was yesterday. It happened on the front porch of our house on Sheridan Avenue in Minneapolis.

Give her your ring, Elizabeth.

And she gave it to me.

*

And, hey; she hated the whole idea of the marriage. That's where the jumping-off-a-bridge idea came in.

Bud—my intended and presumably my *inamorato*—was not a Catholic, and did not want to become a Catholic, and therefore we could not be married in the Catholic Church. By a priest.

So I thought my friend Miriam's father, who was a Lutheran minister, could do the honors. I asked my mother what she thought about that, and she said: I'll jump off a bridge.

Mama! I said. You couldn't do that! You know you couldn't! It would be a mortal sin!

I wouldn't be in my right mind, she said.

*

Hey, even my father, who claimed to be an atheist, turned Catholic for three weeks in order to marry my mother. (And if he hadn't married my mother, I wouldn't be writing this story, would I? Everything connects.)

*

My mother was—well, lots of folks were then—a total, dyed in the wool, died in the will, Catholic. If the Pope said it, it was right. If a priest said it. Forget reason. Forget logic. And for God's sake, forget science. Worse: *deny* science utterly.

When I—little know-it-all snot—showed her a photograph of *Pithecanthropus Erectus* in one of my school books, she said: I don't believe it.

But it's right here! I yelled. In a *book!* A *photograph!*

They could have made it up, she said. That photograph could be a fake....

Arrgh, I said. Giving up on her. For the second or third time. The hundredth time. Stupid old woman.

I thought.

Actually, she was right. They could have faked the photo. And did—I know of no ape-man who was dug up with hair on his body. I only know of bones.

*

I'd have to say that one of the biggest things I've learned over the course of my life, eighty years now, is that I very frequently have to say: You Could Be Right.

Well, look at the thing. Anybody *could* be right. About *anything*. If you take the, you know, like, Buddhist view. The God's-eye view. Or any such.

So I often, these days, have to say: *You could be right.*

*

I had a very hard time saying it about George Bush, though. Until I had a weird dream in which I heard a voice say: over and over, which has to mean that you are supposed to remember it, don't you think? anyway, I heard this voice say: *Laura Bush is an avatar.* Hey. I didn't even know what an avatar was. I finally—after maybe the fifth repetition—got up in the middle of the goddamn *night,* for heaven's sake, and looked it up in the dictionary. *An avatar,* the dictionary said—one of the definitions, the one that grabbed me— *is a manifestation of God.* Laura Bush is a manifestation of God. It put a whole new slant on things—you can see that it would.

In one way of thinking, *everybody*—and maybe every*thing*, I am not quite enlightened enough to say for sure what I think about *that*—anyway, in one way of thinking, basically *my* way of thinking, absolutely everybody is a manifestation of God.

Even George Bush. I still have a hard time with that though. And I am currently having a hard time with Bill O'Reilly.

*

And with Tim Pawlenty, our governor. Minnesota's ex-governor. Have you ever really looked at Tim Pawlenty's face? He looks like a weasel.

*

Listen, that bridge fell in Minneapolis because of his No-New-Taxes policy. What the hell do people think taxes are all about, anyway? Taxes are about services. And bridges.

You don't want your garbage collected? Fine. Don't pay taxes. Haul it off yourself. (You think what you pay covers it? Forget it.)

You don't want your roads repaired? Okay. Bump the guts out of your Lexus hitting potholes. See if I care.

You want bridges to fall? Fine. Don't pay taxes.

I was so proud of our mayor, Minneapolis's mayor, R.T. Rybak, when he said—in answer to the question, who is responsible for the bridge collapse, and all those people dying and getting hurt and getting traumatized, Christ, think of the children in that school bus that as near as dammit went into the drink, into the Mississippi—when he said: Everybody in Minnesota who voted for No New Taxes is responsible.

Up the side, R.T.

*

Elinor was horrified when she heard that there wasn't going to be an engagement ring. She went out and bought me a really beautiful Siamese silver bracelet.

You have to have *something*, she said, something to commemorate an occasion as important as an engagement.

And that bracelet was the one, a few years later, that I put around my first child's wrist when he died, when he was buried.

Everything connects.

*

The title here: "Labyrinth." I have to tell you about that.

The other day I was out with my young friend, Danielle, who is the daughter of my very old friend, and in actual fact my *dead* friend, Maeve; Danny takes me grocery shopping at Aldi's, a discount grocery store we have here, and that I understand they have more or less all over the world. It is very nice of Danny to do this, since a) I don't drive, b) I am what anybody would call poor, and Aldi's is right for me, and c) I am what almost anybody would call old. Too old to shop any more on the bus and carry big bags of groceries, cat litter, etc.

My chiropractor says eighty is not old, I am not an old lady; but between you and me I think she is talking through her hat.

Or whistling in the dark.

*

Anyway. Danielle said, apropos of nothing that I can recall, *I am an atheist.* Well, frankly, I was amazed.

Even her mother, the redoubtable Maeve, whose opinions were always very firm and frequently off the wall, wasn't an atheist. She taught Sunday School in the Unitarian Church, for goodness sake.

You mean that you are an agnostic, I said.

You mean that you can't know whether or not there is a God.

I mean that I am an atheist, said Danielle.

Against God, I said.

"Atheist" doesn't mean that I am *against God,* Danny said.

It means that I totally deny, totally, that there is any such thing as a God.

(There you go, Laura Bush. Out the door. Into the toilet.

(There you go, Mama....)

*

Hey, getting back to Laura Bush and *her* inamorato. I don't even have trouble with *Hitler* being a manifestation of God, for heaven's sake. I acknowledge as perhaps correct what somebody said to me a few years ago: Hitler is in heaven, they said.

Yes, I agree. If anybody is there, he is too.

I said.

So why do I have so much trouble with George Bush?

With Tim Pawlenty?

Maybe it's because they are both Republicans.

I really do hate and deplore most Republicans. Enlightenment will take you only just so far.

*

I hate them because they vote for No New Taxes.

What, a very young friend, a kid, really, asked me the other day, what is the difference between Democrats and Republicans?

It's a choice, I said, between people and money.

I believe that, you know.

But I could—my fucking *teeth* are grinding—I could be wrong.

*

I learned the difference between Republicans and Democrats from Elinor, who was—is—a rabid Democrat.

The other day, over the phone, I said to her: You know, when I was in college, at first, I was a member of the Young Republican Club.

Good grief, said Elinor— pause, puffing on a cigarette, I could hear that on the phone, deep indrawn breath, hold it, then Puff!— good grief, if I'd known that I'd never have asked you over that first time.

She asked me to come for supper to her little apartment in Maeve's house, you remember my dead friend Maeve who taught at the Unitarian Sunday School. I met Maeve through Elinor, Maeve was Elinor's landlady.

Everything connects. Look back on your life. It is like unrolling a ball of string.

*

Remember What's-Her-Name, who unrolled a ball of string (or something, I forget) so she could find her way back from— what? the Minotaur's cave? the underworld?—anyway, so she could find her way back to air and light, from the windings and turnings of a labyrinth. Remember her?

Clearly my classical education is a little lacking. Hey. What do you want from me? I'm an English major and a social worker, for God's sake.

*

For God's sake?

*

I also met Howard Zinn through Elinor. Elinor and Howard taught together at Spelman College in the fifties or maybe the early sixties. At the time the Civil Rights Movement was just getting underway.

You know who Howard Zinn is, don't you? You don't? Jesus. You must be a Republican.

Or an ostrich.

How does Howard vote? I asked Elinor once. Democrat? Green? Socialist?

Independent?

I've never had the guts to ask him, she said. I do know, though, that he is a friend of Ralph Nader, and he *begged* Nader not to run in 2000, but he ran anyway, and look what happened— we got George Bush and the Iraq War.

(You *certainly* know who Ralph Nader is. You don't? Well, wow.)

Looking at it through that lens, you could certainly say that Ralph Nader, the great hero of the common man, which is to say The Consumer, you could say that Ralph Nader caused the war in Iraq.

Shock and awe. And six degrees of separation. By the six-degree rule—that everybody in the world is connected to everybody else if you trace back six layers of relationship—by that rule, I know Ralph Nader. And God knows who Ralph Nader knows.

God knows.

*

Once I got my name in the same e-mailing with Marv Davidov and Marisa Tomei. That was when Howard sent out a mass e-mailing telling people that his wife Roz had died. *I can't call each of you separately to tell you*, he wrote. *I can't send separate letters. It's too hard....*

I printed off the e-mail to send to Elinor, because she doesn't use a computer. So Elinor is connected to Marv Davidov and Marisa Tomei too.

*

And Roz, whom I knew, knew Kurt Vonnegut. Therefore....

*

And why are you a Democrat? I asked Ellie. I know that you think—like I do—that the Dems are almost as bad as the Republicans.

Well, said Elinor. I figure like this: if I vote Democratic, there is *some* chance that *some* money will get down to the people who really need it, and if I vote Republican, there is *no* chance....

*

That's a very fragile thread to hang your hat on, tie your politics to, but there it is, it's what we've got, not a sturdy ball of string but a fragile thread....

*

My friend Deanna, who reads these stories as they are being written, informs me that it was Ariadne (in the Greek stories) who gave a thread to her brother Theseus so he could go to the Minotaur's hideout at the center of a labyrinth on the island of Crete, kill the Minotaur, and then get out again.

So I was close. In my version, there *was* a Minotaur. And a labyrinth. But in the Greek story the person who went in was a guy, not a girl. Woman, pardon me. And the ball of string was a thread.

The Minotaur was this big bull/man who brought people into his lair and ate them, until Theseus did him in.

Who is our Minotaur? And who will kill him?

Remember Pogo? The comic strip? "We have met the enemy and he is us," said Pogo.

*

One day Maeve and I (you remember Maeve, Danielle's mother) Maeve and I went to a Picasso exhibit at the Walker here in Minneapolis.

It was the last day of the exhibit. Up until then we had thought we wouldn't go because a) if everybody else was going, it must not be our kind of thing, it must be totally beneath glorious Us, and b) it was Picasso's private collection, how good could it be if he hadn't wanted to show it while he was alive?

But suddenly: that day: *My God, Maeve, it's Picasso! How dumb are we being?*

I yelled.

So we popped into my car that very minute (I was driving in those days, I don't any more), and drove to the Walker, parked, waited in line for, like, *hours,* and finally got in and trekked in a single line past the art.

The big painting called *The Minotaur* was there. I stood in front of it and suddenly there were tears pouring down my face—I can't tell you any more about it, what it was like or anything, only that there was a flood of tears.

*

Maeve and I cut ourselves off from a lot of good experiences by being snobs: if the hoi-polloi loved it, how good could it be? *My Fair Lady, Dr. Zhivago.* We missed them. But I think the sight of *The Minotaur* changed us. I know for sure it changed *me,* it changed the way I saw things after that. Whether it changed Maeve I couldn't tell you—only Maeve could tell you that, and like I said before, Maeve is dead.

*

Very Few Get Out Alive, my father used to say.

II

The second wedding happened when Bud and I had lived in New Ulm, in Flandrau State Park Group Camp, as caretakers, for about nine years. I didn't entirely realize it, but I was slowly going bonkers, I was becoming a drug addict and an alcoholic, and I think that may in part have accounted for the second wedding.

Listen, we went down there for *one year,* so Bud could write his book about WWII, he absolutely promised *one year* on the very day we were married the first time. When I met him, "fell in love with him", he was an atomic physicist, had studied with Oppenheimer, had been offered a job at the Oak Ridge laboratories. I know he feels that I lied to him about being an independent sort of woman when we first met; but hey! he lied to me too. Suddenly he wanted to stop being a physicist—all atomic physics, he said, were preparation for war—and WWII had turned him into a pacifist.

(I put "fallen in love with him" in quotes because I think the real reason I got married was because I was afraid to get a job. Of course, I believed that it was because I was in love.)

I didn't entirely want to buy the pacifist stuff, I mean, I tend to be a little more aggressive than that personally.

Listen, Bud, I said once. I want to ask you a question. I want to put a case to you. If someone was threatening to kill me or Margaret, would you kill them to save us?

In his inimitable, stuffy, wooden fashion, he said—after a moment's thought, I'll give him that--*I would hope that I would never kill anyone under any provocation.*

Well, lah-di-dah. Hot damn. I had married a total idealist. And I guess that answer told me something about where I stood. And where our child stood. (I do think he was kidding himself, you know. I don't know about me, he claims that he still loves me even now but I just don't know; but Margaret? Margaret is our daughter, and she is the apple of his eye. Anyone who hurts Margaret has to deal with Bud, and I'll bet you fifty dollars right now that he would turn into a werewolf if anybody threatened her and he'd tear their throat out with his teeth....)

Anyway. He found this place in the southern Minnesota park system where we could live rent free just to *be* there, and where he could write his first book, *Ursula.* We had no particular duties there, we were just *there* and were called caretakers by the rest of the park people.

I cried the whole of that first year, I was so lonely, hey, a city girl dumped into the wilderness, seven miles from a town, down a winding gravel road that was snow-covered for five or six months of the year, no phone, no money, no friends?

Of course I cried.

There was my new husband, disappeared every day into a cabin across a creek, writing up a storm.

Well. He finished the book and entered it into a competition and whaddayaknow—*it won!* A thousand dollar prize! A thousand dollars then was at least what ten thousand would be today.

Winning that competition got him Feike Feikema—later Frederick Manfred—for a sponsor. And Feikema got him an agent.

And of course that was so encouraging that he had to start on a new book. In the woods. Where else?

All in all, we lived there twelve years. We went there in November of 1953, shortly after my graduation from college, *magna cum laude*, I'll have you know, it could have been *summa*, but hey! I was cracking up then too; and we stayed there until 1965. The camp was in 740 acres of woods, had a stream running through it, and many buildings, including the cabin we lived in, that had been built by German prisoners of war during WWII.

(Certainly we had prisoner-of-war camps. What do you think happened to the prisoners we took? we shot them all? Hey, we were plenty bad, but we weren't *that* bad. At *that* point we were still honoring the Geneva Convention.

(And you want to talk about ethnic cleansing? Genocide? Think of The Trail of Tears. Think of Wounded Knee. Think of the monument in Mankato, Minnesota, that commemorates the hanging of thirty-eight Sioux Indians—thirty-eight anonymous Indians, they just chose *anybody* for the hangings, no trial by jury, or military tribunals, or any proof of anything at all, any old Indians would do—the hanging of thirty-eight Indians in retaliation for the so-called Sioux Massacre of 1862.

(Hey, read about it some time in some unbiased text. I recommend Howard Zinn's *A People's History of the United States*. For that matter, read about it in the massacre anniversary newspaper that Bud and I wrote for the event. Yeah, we worked for the New Ulm Daily Journal; I'll tell you more about that later. And figure out why the Brown County Historical Society archives are now closed to the public, so that no one can ever again find out what Bud and I found out. You think our hands are clean? Forget it.)

Anyway. Back to the main thread here. Or one of the main threads: when I get going, I do follow lots of threads, lots of sidetracks: that's the way I am. Anyhow: a main thread, the two weddings.

We had a daughter, Margaret, in 1959. And if I thought life was hard there before, having a child compounded the problems of living in the woods.

Margaret had colic for seven months. She screamed her beautiful little head off for *seven fucking months.*

Give one of us something to make us sleep, I said to my doctor, Peter Allenberg, known informally around the town as "the drug-pusher."

You have to knock one of us out.

I said.

First he gave me three different tranquillizers for Margaret. Each of them made her worse. We later found out that she was learning-disabled—Minimal Brain Damage, they called it then— and tranquillizers have a reverse effect on such kids. You'd think the doctor—father of seven kids himself—could have figured that out, wouldn't you? Hell, no.

Finally he gave me a sleeping medication called Placidyl, which turned out to cause brain damage, and which put me into a hospital five years later as an addict.

And Margaret—ADHD, they would probably call her problem these days—was hyperactive as hell. It was so hard to keep track of her. There were the woods, the stream, the Little Cottonwood River, which was dammed during the summer to become Flandrau Lake, the gravel road up to a main county road—I had to protect her from all of these. And hey—the woods were full of barbed wire, and, to top it all, our dog, Jenny, hated the new baby, was jealous as hell. So I had to protect her from the dog into the bargain.

What I am trying to tell you here is that life in the woods after Margaret was born was difficult.

And where was Bud during all this? Why. He was over in his cabin across the creek churning out masterpieces: another book and a play: while I was quietly becoming a drug addict and going nuts.

When Margaret was three years old, I decided that the reason for all my misery was that I had been married outside the Catholic Church. (Well, fuck, you'd have to be inside my head watching the bats flying around in the belfry to understand why I came to such a loony conclusion.)

I made an appointment with a Monsignor in New Ulm. (Sure we had a Monsignor there. We were a cathedral town. We had ordinary priests too, but nothing but a Monsignor would do for splendid me. Christ, was I delusional. Well, I still am, kind of. I still think I am hot snot. Not as hot as I used to think I was, though. And not as often. Maybe I am improving with age. A little.)

We sat in the Monsignor's office. Monsignor Engel, his name was. He was a man about sixty years old, dressed in ordinary priest clothes, you know, black suit, white collar; they save the Monsignor regalia for special occasions. Like the one we were about to have.

He sat behind a beautiful wood desk, I sat in front, like in a shrink's office.

I want to come back to the church, Monsignor, I said.

Which started a fountain of tears.

He handed me a Kleenex from a box on his desk. Ready Freddy. I guess they get a lot of criers in a priest's office.

Tell me about it, my child, he said.

My child—that started the tears again. More Kleenex.

But finally I pulled myself together enough to tell him the whole tacky story: my mother wanting to jump off a bridge, the engagement ring, the ADHD child, the barbed wire, on and on.

Lots of tears.

Lots of Kleenex.

Apparently he was convinced that I was sincere in my half-witted desire to come back to the Church. Actually, of course, I was just crazy. I would have grabbed at any old straw at all, and Coming-Back-to-The-Church was the straw that had bobbed to the top of my consciousness.

But I didn't know that then, of course.

I totally thought that the only thing that could help me was The Church.

Finally Monsignor Engel set up a series of counseling sessions. He wanted them to be for me and Bud together, but I explained that Bud was completely dedicated to his writing and would not tear himself away from it for anything.

Well, at that time Bud was working full time as a reporter for the New Ulm Daily Journal, in addition to doing his own writing. Everybody in town knew him as a completely honest man, and everybody respected and admired him.

Example: One time I was walking in the downtown area of New Ulm and a man came up to me and said: Are you Bud Shepherd's wife?

Yes, I said.

Well, can I shake your hand?

Wow.

People there admired him so much that just shaking his wife's hand was some kind of honor.

Well, wow.

*

Anyway. We had—me and the Monsignor—the counseling sessions, during which at one point he recommended a book to me.

Graham Greene is the author, he said.

I believe the title is *The Power and the Glory*.

Now.

But it was originally titled *The Labyrinthine Way*.

The Labyrinthine Way.

Oh, baby. Right up my alley. My labyrinthine alley.

Of course I got it. Of course I read it. I am reading it again now. It is a story about a "whiskey priest" in Central America, and the twists and turns—the labyrinthine way—that bring him eventually to a wall and a firing squad, and, one presumes, to God.

I am reading it because it popped into my hand in a second-hand bookstore the very day after Danielle told me she was an atheist.

She is going with a guy named Waldo. Waldo? I said. Come *on.*

Yeah, isn't that weird? said Danny. But his interests are a lot like mine. He reads. He cares about the environment. For example. When I told him about my "conversion" to Catholicism, he asked me if I'd read Graham Greene.

Said Danny.

(Yeah, she converted to Catholicism too. And she makes up reasons for it, just like I did for the second marriage. *I wanted to explore my heritage,* she says.

(Her father was a Polish Catholic.)

You know Graham Greene? she said. To me.

I know Graham Greene, I said.

You should read a book called *The Labyrinthine Way,* I said.

*

And that very book just jumped off the shelf into my hand the next day. From The Hand of God? I thought so. I think so. But anybody who knows me will tell you that I am completely over the top on the subject of God.

I call Him/Her/It God because that word is easy for me. I could just as well say *Universe. Nature.* My day is full of prayers: *Dear God, please help me to find my pencil.* That's too small a request for God, you think? Hey, what I think is: Who am I to guess at what God considers small? Or large? Who am I?

*

Hey. Yeah. Good question. Who am I?

I read a book yesterday by a guy named F. Scott Peck, when I was working out in the basement on my Nordic Track. Or however you spell that. (Trac? There's no telling nowadays what they will do with language.) The name of the book was *The Road Less Traveled*. It's the second or third time I've read it.

Scott Peck says I am working to become God.

Hey. I think I already *am* God. Like an avatar. You know? All of us. We just don't get it, that's the problem. Maybe if we did, we'd behave a little better. We wouldn't let bridges fall. We'd have universal health care. For example.

*

Can you believe that this is the only country in the developed world that does not take care of its people?

III

It occurs to me that it wouldn't be fair to let you think that life in the Flandrau woods was *only* horrible. There were good things and fun things too—many.

We really *were* deep into woods, and for me, the city girl, once I pulled myself together, it offered an opportunity for learning of a kind that I had never experienced before. There was a pretty good library in New Ulm, and whenever we went to town I took out books about things that grew in the woods. After a few years, I knew every plant in those woods, its common name, its Latin name, and where and when it grew. The list of favorites is long: the nodding wake-robin—a subspecies of trillium— jack-in-the-pulpit (in all the years I found only three of these in the whole forest area behind our house and across the creek; every year I watched for them, oh, what a wonderful day it was when I found the third one after I'd thought for *years* that there were only two), wild ginger, dog-tooth violets, false Solomon seal, mayflowers, marsh marigolds, on and on.

When we got to New Ulm, it was in the middle of a bad recession, not as bad as the one we are in now, in 2011, but bad enough. There were no jobs. You'd think that would be a hard thing for us, and of course it was, but it also taught us a lot.

First we sold our books. (Here's a hint for you about the solidity of our marriage: on the day after our wedding we talked about how we would divide the books in case we got a divorce....) Then we cashed in my life insurance policy, worth about a hundred dollars. (That was another instance confirming my mother's doubts. She had to give me permission to do it, since she had taken the policy out in the first place.)

Finally we went on unemployment insurance. Bud had worked for a paper company in Minneapolis all through his college years, and so he was eligible. The check would come, I think, every two weeks, (we had to stand in line at the unemployment office to get it, and was that ever hard. For sublime Us? It was hard.) and when we got the check the larder would be down to nothing. *Nothing,* honestly. We learned to shop very carefully to get the biggest bang for the buck; and we would carry back to our cabin in the woods a two-week supply of groceries; and stocking the kitchen shelves with those cans and bags and boxes gave us joy— yes, really, *joy.* I have known that joy in my life, and it was such a simple thing: just seeing some bright-colored boxes and bags and cans, and piling them up, and knowing that we would eat for another two weeks.

Meats—mostly soup-bones, one thing I did know how to make was vegetable soup—we simply put out on the front porch in a metal box. (It had to be metal or the wild animals would get it—hey, I keep telling you, we were *in the woods*). Other freezables too. Perishables we kept in the back room of our cabin, where the temperature was about 40 degrees, over that first winter.

We learned to can things. And we did it together in the little kitchen—jars and jars of fresh produce that we bought from the farmers around, and from the local stores. One year we put up seven hundred jars of peaches, pears, beans, beets, apples. Oh, lord—*apples!* They were made into pie apples (eventually we had an oven, pretty makeshift, but an oven) apple sauce, apple juice, and—from the leftovers—apple butter.

(Those beets--Bud brought home a half-bushel of beets that he had gotten free, and we canned them. What an ungodly mess beets are: leaking permanent red all over everything, our hands, our clothes, the sink. You must love beets, I said to Bud when we were finished, and all the red jars stood there like little red soldiers.

(I hate beets, he said. I thought you liked beets.)

*

Folks—we were *poor.* I'd been poor before, I'd grown up during the Great Depression; and Bud had been poor, he was the son of a mostly unemployed carpenter and town drunk in Glascow, Montana—but this was the first time that either of us figured out that *Poor* could be managed, *Poor* could be creative, *Poor* could actually be fun.

Creative? Oh, yeah. I learned for example to bake during that first winter without an oven. We had two hotplates—free electricity was part of our deal with the Park Service—and a cookbook. I would mix up a small batch of cake batter, pour it into a round pan, set the pan on one hotplate (lifted up on something metal, I don't recall what, maybe some kind of jerry-rigged double boiler, so the cake wouldn't burn on the bottom) dot the top of the cake batter with maraschino cherries, and then hold the second hotplate upside-down above the batter so it could cook from both sides.

Honest to God, I did do this, and the resulting cake was one of the best things I ever put into my mouth. Bud and I took turns holding the second hotplate; our arms got tired pretty fast.

I still qualify as poor—pretty much by choice now. I took to heart what Henry David Thoreau said: *A man* [or woman, I guess] *is rich according to how many things he can afford to get along without.* Something like that. And: same author: *The true cost of a thing is the amount of life you have to trade for it.*

Hey, hey. I *heard* that. I wanted to be a writer, I didn't want to be a worker-bee my whole life. I worked as a social worker eventually only as long as I had to in order to pay up the mortgage on my house, which I now own outright. I have learned to ride the bus—*much* cheaper, and *much* more environmentally-friendly than driving a car. I buy almost everything second-hand.

A friend said to me recently: You are the richest poor person I know. And that's right. That's what I wanted to be. A poor person rich in life. You go, Henry David!

*

We also learned to steal, out there in the woods. We did this under the theory, promulgated, as I understand it, by the Catholic

Church, that to steal food to keep yourself from starving is not a sin. Food, okay. But steaks and maraschino cherries?

Cigarettes? Come on, folks.

*

I taught Bud to steal. I'd done it all through high school. For fun, then. Now for necessity. And I have to say, we were a pretty good team, we got pretty good at theft.

One day we went into a grocery store and followed our usual modus operandi: we got a grocery cart and put a few items into it. We had a little money with us, enough to cover a few inexpensive things: soup-bones, say. Which were really cheap in those days: maybe a dime. Maybe a quarter.

And some veggies: maybe a bunch of carrots. An onion. Potatoes.

Meanwhile we would be tucking other and more expensive items into our clothes. Nuts in a pocket. For example. A little jar of cherries. Yum-yum. We knew we'd have a treat that day: cherry nut cake. My version.

It was so dangerous. Hey, what if we got caught?

It was so much fun.

I got totally carried away sometimes. I'd be doing it just for the thrill.

On one trip I was pushing the cart along and I met Bud—as arranged—at the end of an aisle.

Let's go, he said.

Not yet, I said. I need some cough drops.

(Cough, cough.)

Well, hurry, he said. Please.

A few minutes later: meeting him again: Come on, he said. We have to go....

Just give me one more pass, I said.

Well, all right, but hurry....

What the hell was the matter with him? He looked sort of, uh, *green*....

Finally: Okay, I said.

I'm ready.

And we made our usual exit through the checkout line, asking for a pack of cigarettes at the end, and paying for our little lot.

When we got out and walked to our car and were safe for this time: What's the matter with you? I said.

You look sick....

He reached into the front of his pants and pulled out a package of frozen steaks.

*

I would have to say, though, that our finest moment came, the apex of our career in crime, when we managed to hook a pack of cigarettes right under the cashier's nose. I think we did that just for flash, just for the challenge.

*

But even so, even with stealing, there were days when we had nothing to eat. No more cigarettes.

Once we debated: what would you rather have, a big juicy steak or a cigarette? Much thought. Finally: a steak, I said. A cigarette, he said.

*

One night: What, I said to Bud, is the very least thing for which you'd sell your soul to the devil?

Quick as a bunny, no thought at all: A thousand years of power and influence, he said.

How about you? To me.

No hesitation there, either.

A carton of cigarettes, I said.

Christ, you *are* depressed, he said. Maybe we should go to Mankato.

*

I got into a 12-step program in 1981, maybe ten years after we were divorced. One of the twelve steps says that we have to make amends for the bad stuff we've done. I made a lot of amends—but it was *years,* maybe twenty, before I realized that I would have to make amends for the food we stole.

The stores we stole from in New Ulm were no longer in existence, so I made amends by sending a lot of money to the food shelves in Minneapolis. That kind of indirect amend is okay as long as you are not doing it to escape responsibility for your actions, and I don't believe I was doing that. If I ever acknowledge that I was, well, I'll have to make the amends directly. Or *more* directly. If I can figure out how.

*

I made another amend, or tried to, for taking my mother's diamond ring.

Mama, I said first, I need to tell you that I am an alcoholic. And I am in a program to help alcoholics recover.

Well, good for you, she said. That you are doing something about it.

My mother just astonished me sometimes. I put off telling her that I was an alcoholic for years. Because I thought she'd be horrified.

She was—for years—in denial about my father.

Your father was not an alcoholic, she said to me once.

He was sick.

Because of the war.

He *was* an alcoholic, I said. One of the worst.

No, it was the war, she said.

It doesn't matter what triggered it, I said. He *was* an alcoholic.

And then suddenly: in response to my own declaration: Well, good for you, she said to me.

My mother every once in a while just knocked my socks off.

*

I told her what an amend was, and that I needed to make one to her.

Oh, don't, she said. Oh, don't.

And looked like she'd cry in a minute.

But I plowed ahead anyway. I'm so sorry I let Daddy make you give me your ring, I said. I'm so sorry I took it....

Her face cleared. Oh, that, she said.

That's okay.

Somebody stole it, didn't they? You haven't got it any more....

Yes, I said. I mean no. I don't have it any more.

What did you think I was going to say?

That I needed to make an amend for?

I said.

Oh, well, nothing....

She said.

I still wonder what on earth it was that I did to my mother that I don't know about.

Whatever it was, it was worse than taking her ring; and that was about as bad as I could think.

*

Unless maybe it was that I was ever born. I was such a disappointment to her. She wanted me to be like the women in her family. She wanted me to become a nun, folks. If *that* doesn't make you laugh, nothing will.

There was also the fact that she didn't want to be pregnant at all. She had been told that my father, being as crazy as he was, ought not to have children. And, being Catholic, she used the only approved method to achieve that end. The rhythm system. It didn't work for her and it didn't work for me.

A few years before she died, she told me that she cried the whole time she was pregnant with me.

(Did I need to know that? I didn't need to know that. Folks, you can see that in a way she got her own back. Definitely.)

*

When we moved back to Minneapolis, Bud and I and Margaret, which we did after I was hospitalized for addiction to Placidyl—as I understand it, my psychiatrist told Bud that if we stayed in the woods, I would die as a personality. Wow. Hey, wow. That sounds dire, doesn't it? I thank God for that psychiatrist, Dr. Chalgren his name was, I thank God for him every day of my life. Anyway, we did move out of the woods the following August. I *tell* people that we moved so we could get help for Margaret, whose learning disability was becoming more and more evident; but actually the move was for me.

The winter before we moved—the winter of 1964/65—was incredible.

Everybody local called it: The Year the Dam Broke. It snowed and snowed. I mean, *it snowed.* And *kept* snowing.

And for some strange reason—God having fun?—it always snowed on holidays. Thanksgiving. Christmas. New Year's. Valentine's Day. Easter. May Day. Mother's Day. Yes, honestly, there was a blizzard on Mother's Day, which is always well into May.

That crowned it for a lot of people. There were an unusual number of suicides that year. People that I knew cracked up and had to go into hospitals—including me.

Hey, I *say* it was for addiction, and it was, but it was also because I was having a breakdown.

*

Our road washed out when the snow melted. There was a deep abyss across the top part of the road, so deep that the car couldn't get past it. Nohow. Bud was working at the paper, and every day one of his co-workers had to come out and pick him up when he walked through the woods to get to the top of the road.

And then the dam broke.

The Little Cottonwood River—I think I said this before—was dammed to create Flandrau Lake in the summertime when people wanted to boat and swim—and every year there were floods. Engineers said—after the fact, of course, the truth is that engineers are no smarter *before* the fact than any of the rest of us—engineers said that the river was dammed at the worst possible place, that building the dam where it was was just asking for trouble.

And trouble we got, every year, but that year in particular. That year an enormous amount of snow covered the frozen river, and then it got cold, *really* cold, for a long time, increasing the depth of the ice, and when the ice began to melt it broke up and got jammed in big chunks behind the dam.

Bud was working at the newspaper and covered the story for a couple of weeks.

He would come home to tell me horror stories about ideas people had suggested to break up the ice so the dam wouldn't go out:

One idea was for a couple of guys to paddle out among the ice chunks in a canoe and then blow the ice up. Folks. That canoe would have been smashed into matchsticks in no time, the guys would never have gotten back.

Another idea—equally goofy—was to send a helicopter to fly real low and drop bombs on the ice pack. Hey—can you imagine what would have happened to the helicopter? Or—for that matter—the dam?

Many other ideas—all just as nuts. Shooting sticks of dynamite out attached to arrows. For example. Bud thought it was all just hilarious and reported it so. But it wasn't all that funny to the people. The big flood caused a lot of pain and loss to the people who lived along the river bottom; why didn't they move, since this happened almost every year? Well, it didn't happen *this* bad, they'd tell you. They'd coped other years. But 1965 ended it. That was the year the dam broke.

Bud rushed into our cabin.

The dam is going! he yelled.

We could see the dam from the bottom of our road if we walked out to the riverbed.

He grabbed the phone and dialed the newspaper and the radio station. KNUJ.

The dam is going!

No, not gone yet, but starting to cave in! Big chunks of ice are tearing away the top of the dam and crashing over it!

Here's the story!

Write this down!

And the story went out over the air.

By the next day, when the newspaper was published, the dam was gone.

*

And that decided us, you know. That was the winter that decided Bud to move out of the group camp and back to Minneapolis.

It took a long time for him to decide. I think he was afraid. I think he was scared he wouldn't be able to find a job.

But he got two job offers in Minneapolis: one from the Star and Tribune—as I recall, at that time the Star was the evening paper and the Tribune was the morning paper—and another offer from a public relations firm.

I remember that we walked, he and I, around and around the block in Minneapolis that my parents' house was on, while he tried to make up his mind which to take.

I *know* how to do the newspaper job, he said.

Piece of cake.

I love newspaper work.

But the PR job pays twice as much.

Agonize, agonize.

Love or money.

Eventually he took the job as night editor for the Tribune, and the rest—as they say—is history.

Do you ever look at how our lives turn on such decisions? This? or that? I do—I think about such things all the time.

IV

We got huge amusement out of making—or stealing— Christmas presents.

One in particular I remember: the Do-It-To-Yourself Home Embalming Kit, made for a friend in Minneapolis who had a sense of humor as dark and weird as ours.

We had to come into the open with that one—you couldn't pick up syringes just anywhere. So I asked my doctor for one.

The biggest one you've got, Doc.

He looked a little odd.

I think it was Dr. Kaiser, who later stood up for us at our second wedding.

A syringe? he said.

What for?

So I had to tell him about the DITY kit.

My goodness, he said.

That seems a little morbid.

Yeah, well, it probably is.

I said.

Anyway. He did give me a big syringe. The gift, when we gave it to our friend, was a huge hit.

Maybe I should mention that that friend later died in a mental hospital. So far, however, Bud and I have both managed to stay on the outside. Except of course for my month in the Mankato hospital for addiction. Which doesn't count. In my mind.

*

I think it was Dr. Kaiser who was the Best Man at our second wedding.

But it may have been Dr. Seifert, who was, I believe, a dentist. Whichever.

Whoever it was had just been elected mayor of New Ulm. So you see, over the course of years we had risen in the social ranks in the town: a mayor, a Monsignor.

During the first couple of years we were very suspect. The rumor—I heard—went around that we were Communists, supported by the Communist Party.

They live out there in the woods, and they have No Visible Means Of Support, went the rumor.

What else could we be?

We had to be Communists.

This was the time of the McCarthy insanity.

Countries go mad too, you know, just like people.

*

But after a while I got a job at the New Ulm Daily Journal, a pretty good rag that came out every day except Sunday.

How I got the job was—uh—a little strange. And interesting. I think.

Bud saw an ad for the position of Correspondence Editor.

I can do that, he said.

He believed—maybe still does, at the age of 85—that he could do anything, anything at all.

So he went in to interview for the job. And got it. What the hell: they'd probably never seen anybody as literate as Bud in the whole history of the town.

Well—except maybe the original settlers. They were a band of atheist-socialists from Ulm, Germany, which remains to this day New Ulm's sister-city. Ulm gave a big statue—of somebody, nobody remembered who he really was, but he became "Herman the German" and was the focal point of Herman Heights, a—you could say—ritzy neighborhood.

But anyway, what I was driving at was that those original settlers were smart enough, for example, to plan a town in which the width of the streets, unlike those in many little towns, is still viable 150 years later.

But Bud, as an intellectual in, say, 1956, was an anomaly in the town.

He came back from the job interview looking annoyed.

Did you get the job? I said.

Oh—I got it, he said. But I don't know whether I'm going to go through with it....

Bud! I said. We need the money!

He looked at me.

Seventy-four cents an hour, he said.

Me! They offered me seventy-four cents an hour.

Seventy-four cents!

The upshot was that when Monday came—he was to begin the job that following Monday—he sent me instead.

And hey! they were so dumbstruck at the audacity that they took me on as a substitute for Bud.

You can see the thinking here.

No way would Bud Shepherd work for seventy-four cents an hour.

But it was okay if I did.

I stayed for about two years, loved it, learned a lot; and eventually a job opened up as a reporter-photographer and Bud took that job.

It paid $1.35 an hour, which I guess was respectable enough.

And Bud—never having had a camera in his hands before— did the job brilliantly, as he did almost everything, and ended up years later as night editor at the Minneapolis Star-Tribune, and after that, after we were divorced, as an editor on the L.A.Times.

Things connect.

Look back on your own life and see if they don't.

*

Bud was a good newspaperman. He didn't much like being an editor, took a cut in pay at the L.A.Times after a few years to be just a reporter, and he was really good at that. Well. People trusted him, you see. They'd tell him anything.

Once he won a big newspaper prize for a series he wrote about a crack addict. A prostitute. The prize—I think I remember this right, although my memory is iffy about everything these days— the prize was seventeen thousand dollars.

By that time, of course, we were divorced and Margaret was going to school in Boston to become an architect.

She telephoned me about the prize.

He gave half of the money to the woman he wrote the story about, she said.

I was—as many times before and since—outraged.

He gave eight thousand five hundred dollars to a *crack addict?*
I screamed.

Jesus.

He could have given to *you.* Or something. I mean, what the
hell did he think a crack addict would *do* with that money? A
prostitute?

I yelled.

Yeah, well, said Margaret. You know Dad.

*

You know Dad.
Oh, yeah. I know Dad. Most of what I know is good.
Saintly, even. But exasperating as hell.

*

Another time he worked on the story about the McMartin
family. Do you remember the McMartins? They were a family
who ran a daycare center for kids.

One day, one of the kids accused a family member—or maybe
all of them, I don't recall—of child-molestation.

The cops and social workers quizzed the kids for weeks. The
kids swore up and down and sideways that they had been sexually
molested.

The whole city got into it, and so did the newspaper.
Eventually the newspaper was printing the most extraordinary
gobble-de-gook. The most remarkable crap.

The kids, for example, declared that the McMartins had dug a
tunnel from the daycare center to a separate house to molest them
there. So silly. Why wouldn't they have just walked them over
there?

All through this staggering tale, the only reporter who thought
the McMartins were innocent was—who else?—our Bud.

He was writing stories countering the main stories upholding
the kids' lies—what Bud saw as lies.

Finally he wrote a story about how the whole city of L.A.,
including the L.A. Times, had been duped.

He showed it to the bosses before he sent it to be published.

No, they said. You may not print this.

Well. Red flag to a bull.

Then I'll have to quit, said Bud.
Fine, they said. You're outta here.

*

End of story? Oh, no. Before he packed up and left, he gave
all his notes on the case to a young reporter, who waited until the
time was right and printed—in the L.A. Times—a sizzling story
about how the newspaper and the whole city had gone mad over
the McMartin case.
And the young reporter won a Pulitzer Prize with that story.

*

People and newspapers and whole cities and countries can go
mad. Hey. It's happening again now. Maybe there is madness at
our hearts.

*

Somebody says to you: kids don't lie. Not about things like
this. Yeah? you can say. Tell it to the Marines.

*

Megan worries that she has inherited this flaw from Bud: the
bad timing, I mean. Dad, she says, is always shilly-shallying
around until the right time is past and somebody else gets the
credit. Or the patent. Or whatever.
Do you do that? I ask. Shilly-shally?
Sometimes I do, says Margaret.

*

I have a problem, the Monsignor said, with the two of you
staying together for at least a few days before the marriage.
You can see what his point was—we might, you know,
copulate. Fuck.
Oh, there won't be a problem, I said. Airily.
Bud is so busy, working all day and writing his book all night
that he is practically in a daze all the time, no way would he want,
you know.
I said.
Still, said the Monsignor. There's the Appearance of Scandal.
I don't remember how it worked out.

Whether I talked the Monsignor around, or maybe stayed with a friend in town for a few days.

Me and Margaret.

By that time, Margaret was three years old.

*

Bud *must* have been in a daze to have agreed to this whole project at all.

*

My mother was very dubious.

Mama! I said. I thought this would make you *happy!*

I thought it would make you happy for me, that I should be married in the Church!

Well, it does, she said.

Over the phone. By this time we had a phone.

I insisted on it when Margaret was born. I have always been able to do for other people things I could not do for myself.

But still....

Said my mother.

You know why she is dubious, don't you? said the Monsignor.

Yeah, I said.

She thinks it won't be a good marriage. She thinks it won't last. She thinks that if I marry inside the church, the marriage has to last.

*

She was right to worry, wasn't she? The marriage *didn't* last. There *was* a divorce: I broke my mother's heart over and over again.

Mama, I'm sorry.

Mama, I'm so sorry....

I wouldn't have done a thing differently, but still, I'm sorry.

*

Maybe this would be the place to tell you about how my mother's diamond got stolen. Remember?—I mentioned it earlier.

At that time we had just moved to Minneapolis, and Margaret was having a difficult adjustment. The learning disability had not yet been diagnosed, she was having trouble in school, she was what they call "Acting Out" like crazy. Seven years old, she smoked, she swore like a sailor, she stole.

The few friends she had were other misfits, cast-offs. One of them was the very strange daughter of a professional wrestler who lived a couple of blocks away.

I mean, under normal circumstances I might have discouraged that friendship. But as things stood, I was grateful that Margaret had any kind of friend at all.

One day the two of them came to our apartment after school.

Can we play with the stuff in your jewelry box, Mama? Margaret asked.

Sure, I said.

So they went into my bedroom and were quiet for a long time.

Then: Suzie has to go home now, Margaret said. Suzie has to go home for supper.

Come again, Suzie, I said. It was nice to meet you.

Huh, said Suzie, and left—clumped down the stairs looking and sounding every inch a wrestler's daughter.

Maybe a couple of days later, I looked into my jewelry box and, my God, the ring had disappeared, and so had the little gold watch that my parents had given to me when I graduated from high school.

My ring is gone, I said to Margaret.

My watch is gone.

Do you know what happened to them?

No, Mama, said Margaret.

It had to be one of them, Margaret or Suzie, who took the items. It had to be. I mean, nobody else had been there.

But I was hogtied.

To this day I believe the wrestler's daughter took them.

But I couldn't accuse her.

I wasn't sure.

It could have been Margaret.

*

And besides, confront a wrestler? Accuse his daughter of theft? Not me, guys.

*

But I mean it to last, I said to Monsignor Engel: coming back to the wedding preparations.

I know you do, he said.

Totally taken in by me, he was. And, well, I think the truth was, may have been, that me marrying Bud in the Catholic Church, Bud being, like, the Hero of New Ulm—but that's another story, the story of how Bud got to be The Hero, and I am having enough trouble keeping *this* story on the rails—anyway, our marriage was, would be, a feather, so to speak, in the Monsignor's cap.

*

There was a party at the Best Man's house after the ceremony. Dr. Seifert's house or Dr. Kaiser's. I was wearing a really nice coat-dress for the occasion, dark gray wool, very slimming. In those days, coat-dresses were *in*.

The doctor—Seifert or Kaiser—offered to take my coat.

Uh, no, thanks, I said.

I'll hang it up for you.

He smiled.

A nice man.

I think I'll keep it on, I said.

But he persisted.

You are the guest of honor, he said. You'll be staying a while. You should take your coat off.

Finally: I can't, I said. This is what they call a coat-dress, Doc. It's a dress. I'm just wearing a slip under it.

He—poor guy—he turned a dazzling shade of red.

Maybe I did too.

Uh, uh, he stuttered.

It's okay, I said. A very natural mistake.

*

Margaret still refers to that night as "The Night We All Got Married."

V

Mankato. Remember that I mentioned Mankato a while back in this story? and said I'd tell you more about it? Well, here's more:

(Story? This is a story? Well, what else could it be? It must be a story....)

Mankato was our Mecca.

It was a bigger town than New Ulm, and it was about thirty miles from New Ulm.

Margaret was born in 1959, so we had six childless years when we didn't have to worry about baby-sitters.

Well. Childless in the sense of no successful childbirth accomplished over that length of time. I told you about the little boy who died, and the silver bracelet I put around his wrist when they buried him. And there was a miscarriage. But the point is that Bud and I were alone in the woods for six years.

And dirt poor for some of those years.

And one of us—me—was unspeakably depressed a lot of the time.

Sometimes one of us would say to the other—Hey, let's go to Mankato.

And we would scrounge around to find money for gas and for a movie. (Mankato had *two movie theaters...oh, wow....*) We would go through all of the pockets in all of our clothes looking for change.

Hey, I found a quarter....

I found a dollar! Miracolo!

Some pennies.

And when it just wouldn't add up right, we would collect glass pop bottles—these were pre-plastic days—to turn in for five cents apiece at Domeier's grocery, which was on the road out of New Ulm.

When we had enough—we were off!

All the way to Mankato we would laugh and joke and sing.

Mankato....

Oh. It is still a code word for happiness in my private dictionary.

If there was enough money, we would buy a pint carton of ice cream in the drug store next to the movie theater.

Anticipating, we would have brought two spoons with us.

And we'd sit through the movie—I remember *Marty*, I remember *Mr. Roberts*—dipping our spoons into the marvelous cold yummy treat.

Hey, you're taking too much....

I am not....
You are too....
Okay, here, then, you take some more....
Will anything ever again taste as sweet?
Probably not.

*

Nectar and ambrosia. In heaven. In the home of the Gods.
Maybe. If I get there.

If I can change my spots at this late date.

Change my spots. On the second day after our first wedding,
our first full day in the woods, I was sitting at my sewing
machine—sure, I brought along my sewing machine, in those days
I was a really good seamstress and I simply could not conceive of
life without my beloved Singer. It was—people told me over the
years—a great machine, made in Britain, pre-war, WWII that is; I
had bought it second-hand from a friend, Beth McBride, who was
an even better seamstress than I was, twice as good, but with
maybe half the—uh—taste. Beth decided she needed to graduate
to a Pfaff, so I bought the Singer. Truly a great machine—gave
me no trouble at all for years and years. And sometimes—thanks
be to God, the electricity out in the camp was free—sometimes
that Singer was the thing that kept me sane out there.

More or less sane, I can hear you saying it.

Anyway. I was sitting at my Singer, sewing. I was trying to
make pleated ruffles out of some red fabric to glue—for our
wedding, someone had given us a can of Higgins' Vegetable Glue;
glue to anything, the label said; and I have to tell you, H's Veg.
Glue is right up there in my mind with my electric drill and my
tree-saw, for over-the-years usefulness—anyway, I wanted to glue
the pleats to the bed frame of an iron bed we were using for a
couch in the front room of the cabin we lived in for the next
twelve years.

And I was having a terrible time making the pleats.

Fuck! I said.

Bud heard.

Joan, he said. You know how I feel about obscenity.

Sure, I knew. But, hell, he'd lived with me for a year on the U
of M campus, in Dinkytown, before we'd gotten married.

You know what they say, Bud. I said. The leopard can't change its spots....

I would hate, he said, to think that that would be true of My Wife....

My Wife. The coming pattern of my life rolled out before my inner eyes.

My Wife. Those two words apparently changed everything.

*

But hey. If Hitler can get into heaven, surely I can too....

*

I tried, folks. I tried to change. I became—within the constriction of living in the woods on almost no money—a perfect Little Wifey.

This was—clearly—before Women's Lib.

I devised a method of hiding dirty dishes in the oven so that I wouldn't have to wash them as often—Bud hated to see dirty dishes. And hey, we had to heat the water on the stove—yeah, we had a stove, with an oven, by that time—so it seemed a good idea to use as little water as possible.

I became a pretty good cook. I learned—for heaven's sake—to make the sauce for baba-al-rhum over an open camp-fire: to show off for guests.

One night, when we had an overnight visitor, I went to bed before Bud and the visitor did. Morgan Blum, as it happened: a former writing teacher of ours at the University of Minnesota.

In fact, we met in Morgan's class.

Dear old Morgan—he's dead now. Everybody's dying.

Morgan did everything he could to talk me out of marrying Bud.

Why, um, why are you going to marry him? He asked me once.

Because he's the only guy I've ever met, I said, who is smarter than I am....

Not true, as it happened; but close enough.

Because he is so stable, I said. So sane.

I need that in a man.

I think, said Morgan carefully, that the appearance of stability and sanity in Bud Shepherd may be deceptive....

But anyway. To come to the point of the story. Bud and
Morgan had stayed up long after I went to sleep, and apparently
Bud bragged to Morgan about what a perfectly tamed wife I had
become.

They tested the thesis.

They woke me up at maybe 2 a.m.

Uhhh, I muttered.

Wake up, said Bud.

I told Morgan you made the best pumpkin pie in the world.

I said you would get up to make us one.

So I did.

I got up at 2 a.m. and made a pie.

*

Christ. No wonder I broke down. I was obviously crazy all
along.

VI

The wedding. The second wedding. Bud and Margaret and I
got all dressed up and went to the church.

The Cathedral.

We met the Monsignor in his house, which was adjacent to the
church.

Monsignor Engel was already dressed in his full regalia.

Margaret—who was three years old at this time and who
totally did not know what to make of this whole business of
"getting married": I thought you *were* married, she said—
Margaret gave the Monsignor a dubious look.

Who's da queen? she said. Loud.

I mean, I can't even write it here without cracking up inside. I
am laughing out loud right now.

Who's da queen?

The Monsignor was nice about it. Think nothing of it, he said.
My nephews call me Munsingwear.

*

I had to go to confession on the day before the wedding. The
Monsignor heard my confession. This was still in the days when
confessions were heard in a little wooden closet with a screen that
opened and shut between the priest and the person confessing.

89

Theoretically, both were anonymous.

In actuality, he knew it was me, and I knew it was him.

Bless me, Father, I said; as I was supposed to, according to Catholic ritual; for I have sinned.

Oh, had I ever sinned.

Father—that's what you still call any priest in the Catholic Church, even the pope, *Il Papa*—Father, I married a man outside the Catholic church.

I have had sex with him for nine years.

(I thought—but did not say—every Saturday night with "Gunsmoke" on the radio in the background....

(There was little, if any, passion in what went on between us, me and Bud—it was more like Doing What Was Expected In A Marriage.)

Father, I broke my mother's heart.

I swore, I guess every day for nine years....

Did you take the Name of the Lord in vain, my child?

Oh, yes.

Oh, yes, and I still do. I have certainly demonstrated that in this story up to now.

My child—did you use contraceptive devices?

Oh, God, I'd forgotten about that stuff, how contraception was a sin and all.

Yes, I did, I said.

What kind? he said.

A diaphragm, Father.

I said.

You can't use that any more, he said.

Okay, I said.

I have to ask you to burn it, he said.

Burn it? Did he know how expensive those things were?

I must have hesitated.

Will you do that? he said. Will you burn it?

Oh, boy. This was where the chips came down, all right.

I will, I said. I'll burn it.

Will you promise?

Yes. I promise.

*

I did, too. I burned it in a big fire out at the Flandrau group camp the very next week.

I do keep promises.

But no way did I ever want to get pregnant again—not after the nightmare of Margaret's babyhood, childhood.

Right there was where the Great Conversion broke down. I did burn the diaphragm, but within a couple of months I bought another one. I bought it in Minneapolis, where no one would know me.

*

By that time in the confessional, I had begun to understand what I was renouncing—swearing, contraception, holy Moses!— and I started to cry.

They say, said the Monsignor, kindly, from his side of the screen, they say that tears are the mark of a truly contrite heart....

*

So. That's pretty much it. That's pretty much the path I followed to get to where I am now. My particular labyrinthine way:

The two weddings.

My mother's ring.

The *Avatar* dream.

The bracelet from Elinor.

My son's death.

Elinor, Deanna, six degrees.

Theft.

Margaret.

The pie, the DITY kit.

The dam, the move to Minneapolis. On and on. (This is basically a *catalogue,* isn't it? like the Greeks—or maybe the Romans, I told you my classical learning wasn't so hot—used in their poetry.)

Oh, there was stuff before this, childhood and adolescent traumas and joys and a few triumphs; and stuff after, becoming a writer and a drunk and a social worker, and retiring, and having friends, and learning to use a walker—yes, I'm that old, it does happen, you know, wait a while, you'll see; and making fancy marzipan cookies every Christmas for fifty years, more, but it all led to the same thing, the same place: here. Me. An almost-finished me; I am eighty now, how much longer will I last? How much longer do I have to stay here?

You know what? I'm not going to mind dying.

"Death Panel"? Hey, what a great idea. Sounds okay to me. I'd like it a lot if every, say, six months or so, somebody called me up and said, *Hey, Marie, What About It? You Ready To Go Yet? Next Tuesday? Fine...*

But you know what I'm going to regret? All the stories. All the stories that are still in my head. Look, God: I'm writing as fast as I can. I'm taking as many turnings in the labyrinthine path as I possibly can squeeze in, walker or no walker. *I love the stories.*

It doesn't matter, says God. You don't have to write so fast. This is it: the stories don't die. You die; but the stories don't. And it all—you, the stories—comes to the same place. The wall. The firing squad. Me.

And hey, kid, you're right. Says God. You stumbled on a right story.

Hitler *is* in Heaven.

George Bush will be there too. Whether you like it or not.

And, kid, you are even going to have to put up with Bill O'Reilly.

Oh, yeah, you'll be there too. Get used to it.

MARTY

I keep a journal of my dreams. But long before I began to keep the journal, I had a dream that gives a certain shape to my life still. Even though I never wrote it down, the dream remains as clear in my memory as if I'd had it last night. Clearer—because I don't really remember much about what I dreamed last night: except that in it I was walking freely: and I haven't been able to walk freely now for a long time.

When I woke up, my legs hurt. Do you suppose I could actually have been walking? Why not? It could be. I believe that dreams are real, as real as waking life: so in my mind, it could be.

Hey. Anything at all *could be.* Can you grant me that much?

*

Marty.

It was a very long time ago, maybe fifty years, maybe longer. It was when I was first married, and that was in 1953, and now it is the year 2011. Eleven years into The Millennium. Are you supposed to capitalize Millennium? I'm not sure. But oh! didn't we celebrate the Millennium? Oh, we did! All of us, all over the world—watching celebrations around the globe on the TV.

I think maybe the Eiffel Tower shooting off fireworks from its entire surface was the best. But the London display was pretty good; even though they didn't get the London Eye done in time.

The London Eye, in case you don't know, is a huge, *huge* Ferris wheel that puts you—going up on it—eye-level with Big Ben, the great clock. Well—even higher than Big Ben, my daughter Margaret says. But eye-level with Big Ben is as high as I can think. Without an airplane, that is. Margaret lives in London now, she is an architect there. She can think a great deal higher than I can.

Margaret and I are going up on the London Eye on September 15, when I go to London to visit her.

This is the last time I come, Margaret, I said, when she had finally twisted my arm enough. Get your head around that—*this is the last time.*

The bribes she offered were pretty spectacular. The London Eye, the Globe Theatre, and a week's stay in an honest-to-God *castle* in Scotland: with day trips around the countryside, by hired car, to Edinburgh, to all sorts of places. Folks! An *honest-to-God castle!*

The love of royalty, majesty, in us, dies hard.

Okay, I said. I'll come. But remember: this is the *very last time*....

Will you come again if I get married? she said.

No, I said.

Well, I won't. Her getting married doesn't mean that much to me. I went to London once to see her architectural designs displayed in the Royal Academy—I couldn't miss that, could I? This time I am going because she wants me to see the work she has done on the Tate Gallery gardens, and the Tate Britain renovation. I wouldn't want to miss that. Well, would I?

But marriage? No. Not that important.

A grandchild? Maybe. But no. They could come here.

I am not just a curmudgeon. Not *just.* Though there is something *quite* curmudgeonly about me. But this refusal to travel any longer has come about because a) I never *did* like to travel, I like to stay in my own back yard, my own house, which is in Minneapolis, Minnesota, USA. God, can I believe that my kid lives in *England?*

And b) because I'm getting old. My body is getting old. This happens. Stick around. You'll see. It happens. You think it won't, but it will. Unless you die young, of course, but that's a whole other track.

I don't think I can come, Margaret, I said.

I can't walk much any more. (Well, I can't. I told you about that early on.)

We'll rent a car, she said. We'll fly to Edinburgh and then we'll rent a car there. You won't have to walk.

She said.

You haven't got a driver's license, I said. You let it lapse.

I'll get a driver's license, she said.

Okay, I said. If you get a driver's license, I'll come.

I thought I was safe, you know.

I thought she'd never do it. In some things, she's a terrible procrastinator.

But she did. The last time she was home, which was Christmas and New Year, 1999/2000, the Millennium New Year; her father came too; Bud; I believe we all thought that if on the stroke of midnight the whole world was going to slide off the back of The Great Turtle, why, at least we would all go together— anyway, Margaret got her driver's license during that visit. She borrowed a car from a friend of mine and sailed through the test like, well, like a hot knife through butter.

I *believe* that the thought about the Great Turtle, or its equivalent, was at the back of Margaret's mind when she came home for the Millennium. I know it was at the back of mine. A little tiny bit. Yours? Come on now, confess. Margaret's father, my ex-husband, Bud, disclaimed any such thought. He is a rationalist, always has been.

It was just hell being a mystic married to a rationalist.

I think of myself as some kind of grassroots mystic, you know. I mean, I haven't made a cause of it, I haven't become a priest, or a nun, or founded an order, or anything like that, but still....

And with my bad legs and my plantar fasciitis, there is no way I'm ever going barefoot any more. No *discalced* styles for this old lady.

*

Hey. Look it up. It's a real word.

*

I also think of myself as a sort of Christian Marxist. No Christian alive would recognize me, but I like to think that maybe Christ would. I mean, in terms of what G. B. Shaw said: wrote: *The only trouble with Christianity is that it's never been tried:* with that idea in mind, I think I am a Christian, or try to be. Within my limits. Which are considerable.

*

Marty. Back to Marty. A movie called *Marty* came out a long time ago, starring Ernest Borgnine. It was his first real success, and, for my money, his only one. Bud and I went to Mankato to see the movie.

Mankato was our Mecca at that time. We were living as caretakers in a woods—847 acres—near New Ulm, Minnesota; in the summertime it was a Girl Scout, 4-H Club, birdwatchers camp; in the winter it was almost totally isolated. New Ulm didn't have a movie theater then and the Twin Cities were too far to drive on a whim. So Mankato it was for us—28 miles. We were so unbelievably poor that sometimes when we got the idea that we wanted to go to Mankato to see a movie—generally to relieve our depression, we were also unbelievably depressed, or at least I was, living as a new bride in a crude log cabin in the woods with no phone, no TV, this was actually pretty much before TV. And no other contact with the world for weeks at a time, a city girl? of course I was depressed—anyway, when we went to Mankato, we would sometimes—often—have to scrounge through every pocket in every piece of clothing we owned to find money.

Hey, Bud, I found a quarter!

Hey, Joan, I found a *half-dollar!* (In those days we had half-dollars, I always thought they were very nice, very useful coins, much better than that silly-looking gold dollar they came out with some years ago. For example.)

Joan—that's me.

Six pennies....

And we would get together all the glass returnable bottles we could find and we would stop at Domeier's grocery at the edge of town and turn the bottles in for cash and be on our way to MANKATO!

MANKATO! The word still sends a thrill of anticipation through me, a thrill of hope. Maybe, just maybe, once we have slid over the edge of the known world—just the other side of Mankato—*maybe* we will find an answer, a new world, a better life, a reason for going on. A reason for staying in the marriage....

And sometimes, if we turned out enough pockets, sold enough bottles, scrounged deep enough, we would buy a pint of ice cream and take it with us into the movie and eat it with two spoons, which of course we brought from home.

*

The night after we saw the movie *Marty* I had the dream.

In it, I kept seeing people from my past—high school and grade school, that was really the only past I had at that time. They were all moving in one direction. I asked them where they were going. No one would answer me. They were all dressed very poorly, in thin clothing; in rags; and there was snow on the ground, the air was very cold; they should have been dressed better, those tatters couldn't be keeping them warm enough.

Finally I saw that they were all forming into a long line, a long column, maybe three or four abreast, and marching—well, shuffling, or drifting, more than marching. Moving slowly along. And as they moved along, they sang, and their song became a dirge, in no language that I knew, maybe in no language at all, maybe just sound. Humming, keening, moaning: in unison: a tragic OM. The music they sang, while it was sad, sadder than anything, was also beautiful, beyond my telling. I can compare it to no music that I have ever heard. But tears will come to my eyes even now, remembering that dream-music.

I ran along the edges of the column, plucking at the rags of the marchers. Who continued to pay no attention, just kept walking on, singing their marvelous song. By now it was a long, long column, reaching farther than my eye could see.

Finally a woman dropped out of the column to tell me what it was all about. The marchers were going, she said, to a place on a frozen plane, where a man had lived for many, many, uncounted, uncountable, years. The man's name was Marty.

She told me that we were not on earth, that we were on a far star, an outreach of earth, where people had gone to found a new colony at a time when, by the quirks and quarks and terrible errors of humankind, earth had become uninhabitable.

Out on the plain, this man named Marty had for all these years sat alone and thought. Yes, *thought.* Just *thought.* And his thought was what powered this star, this whole colony of people. His thought gave the star its light, its warmth.

Why are you singing this sad song? I said.

Marty is dead, she said.

And she told me that all these tattered pilgrims were going out onto the plain, which had begun to freeze when Marty died, to pay a last homage to him, to grieve for what was lost. Now that it *was* lost, *now* they understood what they had had; and what they no longer had and could not have again.

Our world cannot survive without his thought, she told me. Little by little, since he died, the warmth has been ebbing. Soon our whole world will die, will freeze. We are going out there to die where he is....

And she slipped back into the ragged column and after a while was lost to my sight. The wonderful, wonderful music went on, swelled and sank, increased and diminished, went on and on. Still goes on in my head, whenever I remember.

And I stood by the side of the road as the singing marchers went by, and I wept for the world that was lost, even though it was not my own world. In the dream, I wept.

*

Years later I talked to a shrink about that dream: Fred, his name was. The shrink's name.

I was in therapy because I couldn't find a reason for my life. I talked and talked about how smart I was, how talented, how squashed I felt in marriage and motherhood. By that time we had moved, Bud and I, and Margaret, who was six years old then, back to the city: Minneapolis. Mankato no longer figured in our lives. The marriage was in trouble. So was Margaret. So was I. I think Bud was making it all right: Mr. Detached.

Fred said: What was the movie about?

I said: It was about a working-class guy, not very good-looking, not very smart, shy, who hung with a bunch of guys who wanted life in the fast lane. These guys talked all the time, bragged all the time, about women they were banging. Or hoping to bang.

Marty didn't have a girl; no girl would have him. He felt like a total loser. But one day he saw a woman—Carol, was that her name? maybe her name was Carol—and she began to interest him. His fast-lane friends laughed at him, told him that Carol was a "dog."

Well. Anyway. In the end Marty stood up to his friends, asked Carol to go out with him, and she did, and they had a nice time. It was understood that the two of them would stay together, would get married and make a life together. It was understood that Marty had chosen a better part than his friends: the way of the ordinary.

*

What do you think the dream means? Fred said. Fred was a little short social worker guy, I don't think he was as tall as I was, and he had the kindest eyes I've maybe ever seen. He was smart; but it was the kindness that shone.

I don't know, I said.

You do, he said.

I knew what he *wanted* it to mean. I knew what I *didn't* want it to mean.

Your unconscious is smarter than you are, he said.

Hell, I'm willing to grant *that.* But what did my unconscious *say?* That's what I still don't get.

Do you think you are ordinary? Fred said. Lay your cards on the table now.

There was a very long pause. Then: No, I don't, I said.

And yet, worry over it as I will, like a dog with a bone, the dream had an effect on me. Still does. Though I claim that I don't know what it means, still, it is *there*, like yeast in the bread.

Although the marriage is over, has been for many years, forty anyway, and I never married again, I still choose the ordinary: over and over. I write stories—not such an ordinary thing to do; no matter in how small a way, it is still the path of the artist, and the artist stands aside and watches—but I write, always, about ordinary people. I write about small events. I value the small and the ordinary. I stay home.

But still. But still. Something in me wanted Margaret to leave me. Something in me wanted her to choose the high road, to *fly.* And she did; she *is;* flying. Can't I have it both ways? Can't the dream mean what it *says*—that the thoughts of an ordinary man— or woman—all the thoughts of all the ordinary people make the warmth in the world?

But maybe the genius is the reason. The genius is born. He— she—has to fly: *has to.* Or die.

I don't know. All I know is that I have chosen my life. I have chosen my path. I'm pretty happy most of the time. I think a lot. I am thinking about you now. I am—forgive me—praying for you.

I believe this is my job in the world.
I am doing my job.
Margaret is doing her job.
What is your job? Do you know what your job is?

THE PARK

It was probably around midnight, maybe even later, maybe 2 a.m., certainly after full dark, and I couldn't sleep. Again. But that night I got out of bed and went to the park.

Van Cleve park, just across the street from the house we lived in then, in the apartment upstairs from Chris and Patty Stavlik, and next door to Amanda and John and Miss Jarvis.

The house which, as a matter of fact, was going to be torn down, so that they could make a—what? football field? it seems to me that they wanted to make a high school football field out of our house; but I couldn't tell you what high school, I don't recall any high school near there. Unless it would have been Marshall-University High? A mile away?

They. They are the powers-that-be, the ones that reach into people's lives and turn them upside down and never know and never care: as a sort of side-effect of *droit du seigneur.* Like the gods of Olympus. Or the god we have now, for that matter, only he is rumored to cause his havoc for good reasons: to teach you a needed lesson, or as part of a Grand Plan that you are too dumb and little and silly to understand, but must simply accept, with or without a smile.

*

I opened the door of the apartment and closed it again, softly. Locked it, so that my husband and my little girl would not wake from the peaceful sleep, the restful sleep that wrapped them, the lucky ones: the chosen ones: those who sleep at night.

(You are just not trying to relax, said my husband. Bud. Often.

(Oh, right. *That's* the problem.)

I crept down the stairs, one slow step at a time, trying not to wake the Stavliks: Patty, who was an ed. psych. student at the University, and Chris, who taught there. I forget what he taught. And their two darling little boys.

Van Cleve park was near the University. Maybe half a mile. A nice walk for Chris every morning. A nice walk for Patty. The lucky ones; who slept; I could see them, striding along the street in the morning, refreshed, rested, full of health and beans.

I, you know, kind of hated them. Such nice people. I really felt like clumping down the goddamn stairs: *clump, clump, clump!*

Oh. But I didn't. I crept down silently. Like a kitty-cat. Like someone who has no right to be in the world. Slip, slip, slip. Slup. Slip-on slippers on my feet. Down, down, down, one step at a time, close to the edge so that the stair boards would not creak. Such a good girl. I was.

I hung the key where we always hung it, in one of those obvious places that every burglar knows, so that a burglar could come right in and murder my husband in his sleep, and steal my child.

*

Across the street, across the grass; the grass already a little damp with dew that would fall heavy later, would be truly soaking and silver by morning.

So dark.

No moon.

"The moon is down...."

Didn't somebody write that?

Who?

I take my slippers off and carry them.

The grass is sweet between my toes, under my feet, just cut yesterday, I saw the mower, just exactly so high, springing, springy, suddenly I can spring up on the grass, suddenly I can touch the moon.

If there were a moon.

There is no moon: the moon is down.

No stars.

I see, as a crowd of looming shapes in the dark, the place where I am headed: the playground, its row of swings, the seesaws, the sand contained in a concrete curb, you have seen a sandbox like that.

The swings are my favorites: they have always been my favorites. Since I was a child. Since my body was a child, I mean; inside I am still a child. I am in my body an old woman now, writing this story for you, remembering how it all happened a long time ago. I wonder if I will be a child inside when an old woman's body dies; I wonder if when I die I will leap out of my flesh prison onto heaven's grass, and bounce up and down, and fling myself onto the grass and roll and roll in the grass, arms and legs flung wide, then tucked in to roll again, flung wide, tucked: so relieved, so happy, to be home again. I wonder if.

*

I crush my slippers into my pocket and choose a swing, push back and forth in it tentatively. My eyes are used to the dark now, I can see another person at the end of the row of swings, I can hear a swing creaking, I can feel another swing vibrating in the ropes of my swing: thrum, thrum. I think it's a man swinging; it is certainly, like me, an adult. Or a nominal adult. He—is it he?— swings pretty hard, considering how heavy he is for these swings, made as they are for children. Maybe he has forgotten that he is not a child in his body. He pumps up, pumps down.

Shall I speak to him? Shall I do the polite thing, just say hello? Hello, *neighbor,* maybe?

Oh, no. No. It would be, it would feel, so intrusive. Wrong, altogether.

I do not speak.

He does not speak, either.

It is like there is a rule about it.

It is like we understand each other, that man and me.

I think it was a man.

*

I can hear your thought: Come *on,* you are thinking, nobody goes alone to a park at night....

But this was forty years ago, and the park was a safe place; just think of it, only forty years ago there were safe places.

Well. Anyway. After that I go back to the park every fair night that whole summer.

I even go back sometimes when it is raining. It's a whole different experience when it's raining. Not better; not that. Nothing could be better than the hot, dark, dry nights, with dew just starting to fall.

But different. As good, but different.

Many people come to the park at night; not just the man on the swing at the other end of the row of swings.

All grownups. All biggish black shapes playing in the dark.

Or in the moonlight. Sometimes there is moonlight. Everything is totally different when there is moonlight. Not better; but different.

In the moonlight I can see the faces of the other people, clear as clear, like they were faces carved from marble. But no one looks at me. No one speaks.

Truly; this is the way it happens. Sometimes things happen that are like this. You don't have to make things up.

*

Miss Jarvis that I mentioned before, who lived down stairs from Amanda and John, was Clarissa Jarvis, PhD. She had taught me Chaucer and Romantic Poets years and years before, maybe ten years, maybe more, at the same institution where Chris Stavlik taught and Patty, his wife, studied.

Miss Clarissa Jarvis was hell on wheels. And a fine teacher. And a royal oddball. She owned the house where Amanda and John lived: next door to us: they had the upstairs apartment and she had the downstairs.

Miss J. claimed that Amanda and John had been sent to her by God, to take care of her in her old age. And they did keep an eye on her: as much of an eye as she wanted kept, which wasn't a whole lot.

Miss Jarvis was the first woman who wore pants at the University of Minnesota. You could say she broke the pants barrier. She never married, but it was rumored that there were affairs; one major affair that went on for many years, like Katherine Hepburn and Spencer Tracy. If you are old enough to remember those folks. Like Dorothy Parker and Robert Benchley.

I suppose the man was married. But maybe he wasn't. Maybe C.J.—Amanda upstairs called her C.J., she said Clarissa just didn't work for such a tough old broad—maybe C.J. didn't want to marry. It would have been like her.

Once when I was her student for Romantic Poets, I ran into her in Folwell, old old old Folwell Hall where the English Department was located in its glory days—when Robert Penn Warren came up from the South bringing with him William Van O'Connor and Allan Tate and Caroline Gordon and Dan Ross. You will know those other names but you won't know the last one: Dan Ross: you should, though, because in his way, which was gentle and laughing, he was as good as the others. Better, if anyone asks me.

He was my teacher too. As well as Miss Jarvis.

Young woman! said Miss J.

To me? I looked around; there was no one else.

Me?

Certainly you, said Miss J. (I can't call her C.J. Not at this point. She was my *teacher,* for goodness sake.)

I don't like what you're doing on my exams, she said.

Miss J. gave little written tests unexpectedly throughout the quarter, Pop quizzes, Isn't that what they call them? The tests were supposed to keep you up to where you ought to be in the reading, which was considerable.

Oh my. She didn't like what I was doing on the tests. Well, I didn't much like what I was doing either.

You're an A student, she said. They tell me. If I give you a B at this point it will be out of the goodness of my heart.

Her voice was high-pitched and breaking and clarion. You have heard voices like that. Just this side of a yodel. She was old already then, close to retirement. She wore the pants she had pioneered, and her gray hair was all here and there, sticking up, sticking out, all over the place, like Big Hair, but an accident, incredibly, rapturously untidy.

I don't believe you've read the book, she said.

And: Have you read the book?

Me: I, I don't have the book....

She stared at me over Ben Franklin reading glasses.

Come with me, she said.

She put her hand under my elbow, hustled me along the hallowed hall of Folwell. We came to her office and she opened the door and pushed me in ahead of her. She picked a book up from a cluttered desk.

Here, she said.

Read it.

Now.

I'm going to my class. She said.

I'm late already. Thanks to you.

She looked at me hard then. What is wrong with you, child? she said. There is something wrong with you.

I gave her a smile, which even to me felt utterly sappy, agape and daft; and which was supposed to explain everything.

Oh, Miss Jarvis, I said, *I'm in love....*

She looked at me as though I had just confessed to having a social disease.

Read the book, she said.

Romantic Poets. Pfaugh!

She said.

A lot they knew.

And she stalked out and locked the door behind her, locked me in to read the textbook. Which I did. More or less. But I nevertheless only got a B in the class. And I still don't know—or like—the Romantic Poets.

*

In the park, the see-saws were left strictly alone. Nobody ever used them during our nighttime play. Well, you can certainly see the reason for this. See-saws need two people, and everyone who came to the playground was alone. No one ever came with anyone else. We were each one of us alone: separate selves, coexisting with others like ourselves, but separate.

Never speaking, never looking at one another, dark and silent shapes in the silent dark, we lived our individual night lives. And who knew what we were in the daytime?

*

They say that C.J. bought the house next door to us for one reason: the downstairs had a big window facing south and she could lie on the sofa and through the window she could watch the stars over Van Cleve Park.

In her later years she was almost completely an invalid. She was badly crippled with arthritis, and she was in pain all the time. She never went out. All day and all night she lay on that sofa in the living room, or sat in a comfortable old chair on a front porch, with a stout cane close at hand, and sipped sherry. Bristol Cream Sherry—no other kind would do. I think, you know, that she was never completely sober. And why should she be?

My husband—Bud—and I, in happier days, and there *were* happier days, it was not altogether a bad marriage, we got Margaret from it, didn't we? anyway, in happier days Bud and I planned what we called The Opium Club. We decided that when we reached an age when we felt that addiction didn't matter any more, say ninety or so, and whether we were still married or not, even if we had to seek one another out at the ends of the earth, we would get together and set up The Opium Club.

And we would smoke opium together for the rest of our lives on earth. Well—in practical terms it's a dumb idea, I mean where are two decrepit ninety-year-olds going to get opium? but in emotional terms it makes perfect sense.

I'm assuming that we will both be decrepit. Well. I'm practically decrepit now, and I am only seventy-nine, for God's sake. We tend to fall apart young in my family. Youngish. Bad genes, my doctor says. It figures.

But surely something like The Opium Club is what C. J. had in mind with her eternal sherry-sipping, lying on the couch and watching the stars wheel—slow, slow—in the night sky over Van Cleve Park.

*

So you could say she had it all worked out, couldn't you? God—clearly—had sent Amanda and John to live upstairs and kind of watch over her; Amanda adored C. J. and would look out for her gladly; and life would go by in its slow wheel, the stars would move across the sky and—star by star—move out of sight as the seasons changed, and then would—slow, slow, night after night—move back into view at the other side of the big window. What constellations could you see out that window?—*I* didn't know, I was young, pretty young, I had no need to know the stars, but what did *she* see? moving, changing, returning, always

different, endlessly the same, slow, slow: the dippers, the Great
Bear, the Hunter? the Pleiades? what?

I didn't know, but she did; that was the important thing. They
say she knew the stars like I know the palm of my hand.

*

And so now the houses across from Van Cleve park, the one
we and the Stavliks lived in, and C.J.'s next door, and everybody
else's on the block—were to be torn down. Amanda—who had
guts and brains and endless stamina—tried everything to get them
to back down. (*Them*—you know *them*, we talked about *them*
before.) Amanda appealed to the City Council, the University
Board of Regents, why, she was even going to call the Star-
Tribune, thinking she could interest them in the story—old lady,
esteemed professor, stars, house, pants-pioneer—but C.J., when
she found out about it, nixed the project.

I have, she said, referred the whole problem to the Deity,
and—such as He is—He can take care of it. Somehow I have
managed to last this long without derailment. I *know* that it will
not happen to me now.

*

Hey, that was all very well, but *my* experience teaches me that
God, except in very rare cases, called miracles, follows a non-
intervention policy. *They made their bed, let them lie in it*—that
has always seemed to me to be His attitude.

Very petty of Him, I'd call it—but who knows what a Deity is
up to?

*

Hey, Amanda—I said from the day we moved in, and as soon
as I realized that Clarissa Jarvis lived next door—do you think I
could go and visit her? Just for a bit? Just to tell her what a good
teacher I thought she was? Thank her? And like that?

Amanda was dubious.

Wait a while, she said.

And: She's not well. Wait until she's feeling better.

Finally: Well, okay.

Instruction: Don't bullshit her. She can detect bullshit a mile off. Be straight. And bring her a bottle of sherry. Bristol Cream. That'll get you off on the right foot.

Remember: no bullshit.

Jesus, Amanda, I said. You must think I'm a terrible fool....

Yes, well, said Amanda. If the shoe fits.

I was a little pissed with Amanda at the time, but looking back at the thing from a vantage point of many years—and I am writing this story many years later, maybe I told you that, I forget things, I am seventy-nine years old now; and will be older; can you believe that that has happened to me? me, the kid? the young woman? who walked barefoot across the grass in the park?—anyway, looking back, I can see that Amanda was right to doubt me, I was and remain absolutely full of shit.

You might be wondering what it was that put Amanda in charge here. She acts like she got it from God on the mountain, doesn't she? Well, there were two things that did it—1) in any given group, Amanda was always the most competent, and nature really does abhor a vacuum, so that Amanda inevitably emerged from any crowd as The Organizer; people—of course, shirkers all—let her do it, and she'd got used to it; and 2) Amanda loved Clarissa Jarvis. Amanda was in charge by right of love.

*

Anyway, I went in to see C.J. one day with Amanda, who insisted on a formal introduction.

I want you to meet Joan Shepherd, she said to C.J. May I present. And, Joan, this is Miss Clarissa Jarvis, the great, the famous, the fabulous....

For goodness sake, said C.J. Don't you think you're overdoing it a little?

Hoot, hoot, yodel.

Not a bit, said Amanda.

Impossible, said Amanda.

Hello, Miss Jarvis, I said.

I'll leave you two alone, said Amanda, though she clearly didn't want to.

Sit down, my dear, said C.J.

To me.

Amanda gave it up and darted off and out the front door and up the stairs with her usual manic energy. We could hear her feet pounding—bang, bang, bang—up to the apartment over our heads.

Amanda is very—headlong, said Miss Jarvis.

You can, uh, say that again, I said.

I have never in my life felt more uncomfortable. I felt set up by Amanda, scared to death; I felt like I was meeting the queen, and I didn't know the first thing about how to behave. I sat down in a wicker basket chair, pulled it toward the couch where the old lady lolled.

I feel like I'm meeting the Queen, I said. Amanda coached me, you know. I'm thinking that maybe the curtsey should come in here somewhere. What do you think?

Hm, said Miss Jarvis.

Uh. Raillery not the right track, I saw. Gentle good humor not okay.

I remembered the sherry.

I've brought you some sherry, I said.

Bristol Cream.

Coals to Newcastle, you know. I mean, there was a *gallon* of the stuff sitting by the sofa.

Lovely, said C.J. My favorite. Amanda told you?

Yes, I said.

Open it, said Miss Jarvis. We'll both have a sip. Well. We both had half a bottle. Apiece. And Amanda was right. It eased things considerably.

I managed to cut the bullshit to an acceptable level, and to avoid all bad subjects, such as eviction.

*

John—John Robinson Harris—who was Amanda's husband, was also a professor, like Chris, but not at the University. He taught English Lit. at St. Thomas College across the river: in St. Paul: Minneapolis and St. Paul, you probably know this, are built on opposite sides of the Mississippi River in Minnesota. John and Amanda were both originally from the South, John from Alabama and Amanda from Tennessee. Nashville, if it matters.

Amanda was very smart and very talented, in an organizational way, as I said before. She had attended Agnes Scott, the Vassar of the South, and had been chosen after her graduation as assistant dean of students. "That time when I was deaning it," she always said, making some fun of it. I do think she was in a way proud of it, though, you know, because she managed to weave it into a lot of conversations.

What she needed John for, I couldn't imagine. Maybe sperm: they had two little girls, Francine, who was three, and the baby, Lily. Well. Maybe she loved him. I consider that explanation unlikely, but possible.

Why don't you leave? I said, many times: if you are so unhappy with John?

Why don't you get a divorce?

I can't, said Amanda.

I am dependent upon John emotionally.

She said.

What the hell does *that* mean? I said.

If you *were* it, you'd know, said Amanda. Waving her hands like a mad conductor with an invisible orchestra.

I'm not? I said. Amused and fascinated. As I always was amused and fascinated by Amanda. And really *interested,* you know. She was so smart, so intuitive and acute, so funny.

She'd call from next door: Hello, Sunshine, she would say. I'm going to the post office. You wanna ride shotgun? I always said yes, if I could.

No, said Amanda. You're not. Emotionally dependent, she meant. You are one of the most emotionally independent women I have ever known. She said.

And I didn't know what that meant either.

But maybe she was right. Since Bud and I have been divorced now more than twice as long as we were married—nearly forty years—and Amanda and John are, for better or worse, still together.

(Amanda is absolutely crazy, says Patty, whom I still see now and then. Truly. Clinically. They're both crazy. They get crazier every year....)

Oh, Amanda: madwoman, magic woman, interfering angel—I wonder if you know how much I have missed you.

*

We were all notified in early spring, maybe March, that the houses were to come down in September. That gave us six months to relocate. This was easy for all of us except C.J.

I am not going, she said.

And: No. No. No. Absolutely not.

In that clarion croak.

Amanda tried and tried to get C.J. to see reason: to let her—Amanda—look for alternative housing early in the six-month reprieve.

There's a perfectly marvelous senior citizens' complex at Ebenezer, she said. Overlooking a little park. I'm sure that if we pulled some strings we could get you a two-bedroom setup.

Amanda. Said C.J. I am not a senior citizen. I am an old woman.

And: Bite your tongue, she said.

And: No, no, I appreciate what you are trying to do, but it simply won't be necessary.

Amanda knew that it *would* be necessary. If there was one thing Amanda knew truly, in the deepest places in her heart, it was that the mills of the gods grind.

*

As Spenser observed somewhere—not the poet, Edmund, but the detective, sort of detective, in Robert Parker's crime novels; I think Miss Jarvis would have absolutely adored Spenser; as she adored Peter Wimsey and Albert Campion; her car, when she had one, was named Lord Peter, and her dog, whatever dog was current in a long sequence of small dogs, was always named Albert Campion—anyway, as Spenser said: the ways of the Lord are mysterious, but seldom pleasant.

*

Miss Jarvis taught me to appreciate murder mysteries. I bought many of hers at the sale they had after her death. I bought all of her Marjorie Allinghams and all of her Dorothy Sayers, and they have been good friends to me ever since. It seems to me that if you have murder mysteries and/or baseball in your life, it's enough—you can then get through okay no matter what else is happening.

*

Amanda had creativity like a kind of genius: all by itself, even though it was never channeled into a form, it was genius.

Unless her form was life?—the living of life?

One day that summer in Van Cleve Park they had, for the little kids, ages three to ten, a decorated wheeled vehicle contest. Margaret was seven then, and Amanda thought she should enter the contest. I can't, Amanda, said Margaret. I haven't got a wheeled vehicle.

She didn't, you know; Bud was so worried about her getting hurt that she had never been allowed to ride a bike. But a limitation of that sort could never stop Amanda; ideas gushed out of her like water out of a pure mountain spring: splash, splash, and there they were, ideas lying all over the ground and flowing down the mountainside.

We'll decorate the carpet-sweeper. Said Amanda.

Margaret looked stunned. That's not a wheeled vehicle, she said.

It could be, said Amanda. It has wheels. You *could* ride on it.

Listen. It's a wheeled vehicle if we say it is. Said Amanda.

Well. Margaret adored Amanda, but this was, you can see it, crossing the line here; this was over the edge.

No, Margaret said. I don't think so.

But Amanda was already darting out of our apartment and clattering down the stairs and into her house and up her stairs to get crepe paper and tape and what-have-you.

She came back a few minutes later with a big collection in a box, and then proceeded to turn a humble carpet sweeper into an incredible, terrific, super-duper production.

She turned it into a giraffe. Honest-to-God. It took hours. It was great fun. We all got into it, me and Amanda and Margaret, Patty when she got home, and even Bud and Chris, when they each got off their respective jobs.

Bud worked at the Star-Tribune. I guess I didn't tell you that. He was an editor. He was not the kind of person to get involved in turning a carpet sweeper into a giraffe.

But: Here's a thing for the head, he said. Sacrificing an oatmeal box, dumping the oatmeal into a brown paper bag. *Marvelous!* Amanda shouted, and Bud the Taciturn began to twinkle, positively.

Why couldn't I ever make him look like that?

Eventually Margaret got caught up in the headlong rush; eventually she allowed as how it was maybe a fairly good idea, and not just a clear embarrassment.

But: No one else will have a carpet sweeper, she said.

Precisely my point: said Amanda, beaming like a crazed sun. Her dyed blond hair stuck out in wisps, like strange sunbeams. *No one else will have a carpet sweeper.*

The next day at the park, the wheeled vehicles and their owners lined up.

What's that? said a bike rider to Margaret. It's a, it's a, giraffe, said Margaret, hanging her head, looking at him sidelong.

But what is it under the giraffe, said the kid.

It's a carpet sweeper, said M.

A carpet sweeper isn't a vehicle, said the relentless little shit.

I saw Margaret's head come up, and I saw Amanda suddenly looking out of Margaret's eyes.

It is if I say it is, she said.

*

I heard recently that Amanda's daughter Francine is now a traffic-planning engineer in Chicago.

*

Well. When the carpet sweeper took the field, rolled out ahead of Margaret, the giraffe gliding backwards, well, it had to of course, I mean, think about it, there was for a second a silence. Then: Dig the carpet sweeper, someone said, loud.

There was a bit of scattered applause while the terrestrial minds took in the idea. Then a roar of approval. Well. As big a roar as you're going to get in a neighborhood park on a Tuesday afternoon.

Up the carpet sweeper!
Ride 'em cowboy....

And Margaret's flag of brown hair flew out in the wind and flags of brown and yellow crepe paper danced off the giraffe in the wind.

It won first prize, of course it did.

And M's head came higher and higher, her eyes sparkled like the stars that would move that night over Van Cleve Park.

We won first prize, she said. To Amanda.

'Course we did, Sunshine, said Amanda. Did you ever doubt it for a minute?

For a minute, I did, said Margaret.

First prize, she said. Wow.

*

On the nights when I went to the park in the rain, it was like a different world.

For one thing, not as many people came when it was raining. Sometimes it was just me and one or two other people.

Sometimes it was just me.

I liked it when it was me and a couple of others, and I liked it when it was just me.

I would sit on my swing, and the seat and the ropes would be slippery with pelting rain, and I would swing, up and back, up and back, and on the upswing I met the rain face on. I swung into rain and rain streamed over my face, and on the downswing, backswing, I fled from the rain, and it was like the sky was weeping; or it was like the rain was inside of me, and the rain was tears.

Afterwards I walked, barefoot sometimes, sometimes in wet shoes or slippers, across wet grass, and across the street and into the house, up the stairs, squish, squish.

*

C.J.'s dog. Clarissa Jarvis's dog. Albert Campion. The Albert I knew was a small dog, old and sick. He had some sort of doggie seizures. "Fits," people called them then. Miss J.'s dog has fits, they said.

Albert separated the sheep from the goats, so to speak, in Miss J.'s classes. She brought him with her sometimes into the classroom; and he slobbered and belched and crept under students' chairs. Slept. Or had fits.

One day she brought him into our Romantic Poets class.

This, she said, indicating the quivering mangy blob trembling at her feet, is Albert Campion. And then she went right ahead with the class.

Well. I have to be fair. I don't really suppose he was mangy. I mean, C.J. was very good to her dogs, very conscientious.

That day Albert C. chose to sleep, or whatever he did, under my chair. He also chose to have a fit. I ever afterwards figured that it was all directed by God: mysterious, useful, but not altogether pleasant.

There was—in the middle of "Ozymandius"—suddenly a tremendous thumping and bumping. I lifted my feet in response to pressure on my ankles, and old Albert Campion came rolling out to rest, if you could call it resting, he was heaving and drooling and twitching all over, at my feet: and—thank you, God, for the inspiration—I reached down and put my hand on his side. There, there, poor Albert, I said. Good little doggie.

Sweet doggie. Pat, pat.

There, there.

Well. You know the drill.

I got a B in the course instead of the C or D that I plainly deserved.

They say she did it on purpose. They say that students who flinched had their grades lowered half a step. If you were a B+, you got a B. If you were a C-, you got a D+.

*

Amanda managed to get a stay of execution for our houses— six more months, we now had until April of the next spring to move.

See? said C.J. I told you everything would be all right.

Triumphant hoot. Superior croak.

Yeah, said Amanda. Okay.

In private, Amanda practically wrung her hands.

What am I going to do? she wailed.

With her? About her?

I don't believe there is anything you *can* do, Amanda, I said.

She's stronger than you are.

And maybe she's right.

Maybe everything *will* be okay.

Sure, said Amanda. Maybe God will do a miracle. Just for me.

Maybe not for you, Amanda, I said.

Maybe for C.J.

I mean, she's certainly the type. Confess. Doesn't she now and then remind you of somebody like, you know, Judith, or

somebody, pounding the nail in the guy's head? Moses, or
whoever it was, parting the Red Sea? One of those old guys?

You can see that my Old Testament education is as rocky as
my education in Romantic Poets.

Well, and there *was* a miracle. Of sorts. Mysterious, but not
pleasant. As an answer to prayer, it left a lot to be desired.

One day Amanda heard a crash downstairs, and then a cry.
She raced down the stairs, let herself in—she had a key, C.J.
trusted her totally—and found C.J. lying on the floor half-way
between the sofa and the bathroom. Her cane was under her. The
crash had been C.J. hitting the floor, plus the overturning of a table
covered with piles of books.

From next door I heard Amanda scream: Oh God! Oh God!
and I came running too.

Oh, C.J., are you broken anywhere? Amanda cried.

No, dear, I think not, said C.J. From the floor.

I took the books and the table off her and stacked the books
back on the table while Amanda felt C.J. all over, limb by limb,
and indeed, nothing seemed damaged.

But when we tried to get her up off the floor, we couldn't. I
may not have told you that C.J. was a pretty large woman, not fat,
but tall and big-boned, heavy; and we simply could not get her up.

*

Eventually, of course, we had to call an ambulance to take her
to a hospital. At first she protested that it was not necessary, she
could just lie on the floor there until she got her strength back,
Amanda could get her a pillow and a blanket.

But finally: It won't do, will it, dear? she said.

I won't do.

No, said Amanda. It won't do. You won't do.

*

She never came back to the house across from Van Cleve
Park. At the hospital they thought she might have had some sort
of stroke. She didn't get any better, in fact she got worse and
worse, and after a while the hospital released her into a nursing
home that Amanda had found. Amanda's most important criteria
for choosing the nursing home were two: 1) Would they let C.J.

have sherry? (Yes, but only with meals and with a doctor's order) and 2)Was there a south-facing window? Could you see the stars?

*

But even the stars and the sherry weren't enough. She lived for only about four months in the nursing home. She lost her wits entirely toward the end; rambled and raved; Amanda visited her as often as she could, and each time when she came back she sat in my apartment and cried and cried.

It's so pitiful, she said.

It's so sad.

That wonderful intelligence gone, all gone, all that wit, everything....

Amanda was with C.J. when she died.

*

Do you remember Young-Quinlan? The department store downtown. YQ was the fanciest such store in Minneapolis. There was a chair inside the south entrance where one could sit and wait while a friend shopped. Or one could make arrangements to meet someone there.

Pick me up at Young-Quinlan....

Or: *I'll wait for you in the chair at Young-Quinlan....*

The chair—in my memory—was as elegant and graceful as the rest of Young-Quinlan. It was carved and curved dark wood, lovely, and had a gold-brocaded padded seat and back: wonderfully comfortable. C.J. died believing that she was sitting in that chair waiting for her lover.

He'll be here soon, dear, she said to Amanda.

He's almost never late....

Never very late....

I wouldn't want a friend who was habitually late, would you?

Hoot. Toot. Yodel.

But soft now, weak.

Die.

*

The night before we had to leave our house—the demolition was scheduled for the next day—I took Margaret to stay with my parents on the other side of Minneapolis, the north side, which was in those days a good solid family neighborhood; and I gave a party. We had already moved most of our stuff out, the apartment was nearly bare.

As a matter of fact, Bud had moved all of his own things out; we were just at the beginning of divorce proceedings. Well, I told you before that it was going to happen. Remember?

Estranged. You could probably say that's what we were. But estranged or not, I still invited him to the party. It seemed like he belonged, whether we were together or not.

It's a demolition party, I told people.

Bring anything you have. Sledge-hammers. Regular hammers. Axes. Whatever.

Well. When they got there, people needed some encouragement to get to the point where they were willing to actually break anything. As a matter of fact, they all had to get fairly hammered themselves before they could do it.

Amanda took the first swing. She picked up a sledge-hammer and swung it with all her strength and the wall cracked. A little. Those old houses were built pretty solid. The second swing broke out a hole between two uprights.

Why. Amanda began to swing that hammer as if she was born to it.

Come on, folks: she pushed out between clenched teeth.

Get in—huff, puff—*ahead of the wrecker!*

Smash.

Get in ahead of God!

Come on!

Try it!

Bang. Crash.

You'll like it....

And oh my, we did like it. Finally everybody got into it, and we destroyed the whole inside of the house.

Swing.

Crash.

Crumble.

Kitchen. Living room. Bedrooms. Bud's office.

You could tell who was sitting on anger—they swung with such enthusiasm. Their eyes lit with such glee.

Well. All of us. Amanda. John. Me. Bud. Patty. Chris. Some other friends: we did have other friends. I served fishhouse punch: you can't go wrong on fishhouse punch.

Swing.

Crash.

Bam.

Wonderful.

And timed just right, I've always thought, to prevent a group nervous breakdown.

*

Toward morning, those who could navigate went home, and the rest bedded down in the rubble or went next door and slept on C.J.'s floors, where the threadbare carpets were all that remained.

As for me, I went across the street to the park. It was April, just beginning to be warm, and it was raining a little.

April showers.

Like they say.

I took off my party shoes, carried them. What kind of shoes does one wear to a demolition party? Spike heels, what else? I walked across the grass, wet with the rain. When I reached the swings, one other person was there: a woman this time. I did not speak to her; nor she to me.

I wondered where C.J. was: in the universe: and I thought, it's not such a bad way to go. Sitting on a brocaded chair in YQ, knowing that your lover will come soon. Knowing that he's almost never late.

What would it be like, I wondered, to be married to a man that you could count on to be on time? Or not married to him, depending on.

I cried in the rain for all of us, and the rain was tears.

*

They never did make a football field, or anything else, out of the block where our houses stood. The houses all came down, as scheduled, the day after the party; and a fence was put up around the block so that kids couldn't fall into the basement holes and get hurt; eventually the ground was filled in and leveled, and grass grew; but a playing field was never built.

So I guess you could say it was all for nothing, couldn't you?

And yet. We did live there for a little while: me and Bud and Margaret, Amanda and John and Francine and the baby, Chris and Patty and their two darling little boys. C.J. And everybody else on the block. We did see the stars there. We did play in the park. We walked in the grass. You really can't expect a whole lot more than that.

We were alive for a while there; and we had the park, we had the grass and the playground, we had the stars; and—for a while— each other.

THE REMEMBERER

I

I was sitting with my friend Maeve in a booth in the Cafe di Napoli in Minneapolis—a place where they have, or at least had at that time, good service and the best vodka martinis in town. On a couple of the latter, we were discussing life, death, and ourselves.

Maeve said—"The thing I always remember that somehow characterizes you best in my mind is that time in New Ulm at the parade when the flag came by, and Margaret fell flat on her face, and you cracked up."

I said—"I don't remember that."

She—"Oh surely you do—it was in New Ulm, when you all lived in New Ulm."

Me—"No, god, Maeve I absolutely don't remember that."

She—"I do. The thing about it that was so great was that it was such a perfect thing to do, her falling flat on her face when the flag came by, so perfectly comic, and you were the only one who saw it...."

Me—"But I absolutely don't remember...I don't remember *one thing* about it...my god what else don't I remember?"

I was really freaked out on this. You can see the problems: *If I don't remember, did it happen? If Maeve remembers, does she have a piece of my life that I don't have? What is my life? Is it what happened, or what I remember?* Jesus. I mean, the whole incident was small, god knows, but it was significant. I mean, it was Maeve, my best friend, the person who understands me best in the world, and she said it was to her the most important thing she knew about me, *and I didn't remember*.

I could see the humor in the recalled incident, but I could also see the other side of it: what happened to Margaret?

"Listen," I said, "maybe if you could tell me some more about it."

She did; she told me that it was a Fourth of July parade in New Ulm, Margaret was about three or four; and Margaret, hyper as always, was running around and jumping up and down, and just as the flag came past us she tripped on the curb and fell flat in front of the flag, in uncalculated obeisance, involuntary and innocent worship. All the people around us were concerned for Margaret, picked her up, tried to find out if she was hurt, etc., etc., and I, *this child's mother*, was off in a corner of this memory somewhere, *laughing because a child falling down was funny to me*.

I mean, can you get into this with me? In a situation which I don't even remember, I behaved like a perfect monster, in my opinion. And Maeve, who remembers it, thinks it is hilarious, in fact the most distinguishing thing she remembers about me, a paradigm for my character.

I should be *arrested*, for god's sake. And here is my good and dear friend, sitting across from me, and she is smiling in profound approval at this really awful thing I did, thirty years ago or so.

But, you know, it *was* funny. The more I thought of it, the funnier it hit me. It just crept in on me, seeped in more and more, and finally it took over my whole mind. I sat in the di Napoli and roared with amusement. And Maeve laughed with me. We just got into it, choked, whooped, wept, had a marvelous time appreciating the terrible humor of something I did that I don't even remember. The conclusion is plain: *I am still a monster*.

"Christ, Maeve," I gasped, when I could. "Do you do this very often?"

Well, yes, she said, she did. She often remembered things that other people didn't remember. In fact, she said, it sometimes seemed to her that she remembered almost everything that has ever happened to her and to everyone else she had ever known and everything that had ever been told to her.

"The Rememberer," I said. "God. Christ."

Maeve smiled, a secret, knowing smile that I see very often on her face.

"It should be a story," I said. "I could write a story about it."

"I think you should," she said.

"You know what would have to happen at the end of the story, don't you?" I asked.

"She would have to be crucified," said Maeve.

"Yes," I said. "She would have to be crucified."

II

In a small town upriver, one of the residents was in a way a sort of magician. This magician was a woman, and people came to her to consult on various things. She was, apart from being a magician, quite an ordinary sort of person. She grew a wonderful garden, a wild garden—anything at all would grow for her, and she spent many hours planting, transplanting, arranging effects which to her were beautiful.

There was a rough, handmade clay jar with a cover on it hidden among the roots of a great tree. No one knew what kind of a tree it was, it had died many years before and all the branches had been cut off; it towered in its essence, a giant, naked trunk. The jar was called a Bad Thoughts Jar—you could take the cover off and put your bad thought in and then put the cover on again and leave the bad thought there in the jar. People laughed at the silliness, innocence, of this notion until they tried it; once they found out that it worked, they stopped laughing.

There was a sand-cast owl caught in macramed ropes nailed to the tree.

The woman was alone a great deal of the time. Her friends considered her an artist, though she had no particular art form that she followed. But things around her became beautiful. People came to feel more beautiful, became more interesting to themselves, when they knew her—because she perceived them as interesting and beautiful. She came to understand that her life and her perceptions of people were her art—she became, as she grew older, confident in her art. She was happy when she was alone and she was happy when she was not alone. She did not, as far as anyone knew, pray to any god; but there was about her a quality of prayer that was present in everything she did, every hour she spent.

She had a talent, a trick of memory, that would come out unexpectedly with the people she trusted. She could remember things about them that they couldn't remember. "I remember," she would say, out of nowhere, "the time long ago when you came and planted azaleas in my garden...." And the other person would not remember, and would go away feeling very subtly strange and changed and wondering. And somehow, sometimes, angry—feeling robbed of something.

She did not do this deliberately, it simply happened that she revealed her memories as it happened that she became able to remember. In the beginning I suppose it felt very safe to her.

But gradually she remembered other things and told them too; perhaps it was at this point a little out of her control.

Eventually it became somewhat ritualized. People came to her more or less on an appointment basis and said, What do you remember about me? and she would tell them.

At first the memories were rather commonplace but then they became strange and impossible.

"What do you remember about me?"

She would laugh. Her laughter would be gentle, apologetic. "Well, I remember the time you threw a stone at a blind child; you were drunk, of course, so it hardly counts...." The person did not remember this, and became very upset. But the artist-woman-magician stuck to it, and would not unremember; she had a great flaw, she had a kind of integrity. People knew she did not lie; indeed, hardly knew how to lie. So somewhere in themselves they had to believe they had done these things that she remembered.

Things went from bad enough to much worse.

"What do you remember about me?" someone said one day. (You would have thought they'd have had enough of it by then; you would have thought they would leave it alone; but it was as though they couldn't; apparently the curiosity of people to find out about themselves is insatiable when the opportunity presents itself.) The magician's eyes grew luminous and her voice was like an embrace—"I remember that you were at Ravensbruck, and that as I walked toward the gas chamber, you pushed me on my way...."

"What do you remember about me?" a woman said. The artist-woman-magician's eyes filled with love, and her voice became warm, accepting. She laughed again, and her laughter was like pure spring water, bubbling with amusement. "You?" she said. "I remember that you drove a nail into my hand when they hung me on a cross. Of course, it was a long time ago, heavens, don't worry about it, I did the same to you...." She held her arms out to embrace the woman, who fled from her in understanding and horror.

*

So of course they crucified her. One night, at midnight, at a crossroads. Upside down. When she was dead they buried her by the crossroads. Buried her good, this time; they drove a stake through her heart as she lay in her deep grave—they all had a hand at driving it in. And they filled the grave, covered her, with iron horseshoes; they were taking absolutely no chances this time. If they had thought of a silver bullet, they would have sent it through her dead skull.

They recorded it in their minds as a suicide, which in a way of course it was. And after a while they forgot her.

But another Rememberer came. There is always one, somewhere. You?

Be careful. Be careful.

PROPHECY

All I've got this time is a title. And even that is not what it should be: I think it really should have been "The Prophet." But you can understand that I couldn't have that. I mean, that title has been taken. Copyright or no copyright. I might as well say I'm going to call my story "Uncle Tom's Cabin." Taken is taken.

So: "Prophecy."

Well, but I also have a character, now that I am thinking about it: Vange. Remember her? I have told you about her before.

I told you she was a blind social worker. A teacher. A Buddha. A worker of rehabilitation miracles.

She is also a prophet. Sort of a prophet. She'll tell you the future if she's in the mood: or whatever piece of the future she thinks you ought to have.

Dark stuff, death, illness, she mostly won't tell you. She mostly keeps dark stuff to herself.

She does her thing with any prop at hand: ordinary playing cards that she reads as gypsy cards, a crystal ball, sometimes dreams.

Once she dreamed that Annette's new husband—Annette was our secretary in CRS, that's Community Rehabilitation Services, which is a department at the Minneapolis Center for the Blind— Vange dreamed that Annette's new husband died of a heart attack.

Randy, his name was. And, as a matter of fact, randy was his game too.

Vange was very upset by the dream, and she pledged me to silence.

Her voice shook a little and her hands trembled as she waved them around the way she does: like she's weaving a net of light, of air.

Sometimes she is a little like a spider in that way: in the way of weaving a web. A fairly benevolent spider with big round eyes: the thick glass spectacles that sit on Vange's nose.

Don't tell anybody, she said. About the dream-prophecy, she meant. You have to promise me that you won't tell anybody.

Well, sure I will, I said. I mean, I'll promise. But you know what my promise is worth, Vange.

The thing is, everybody knows that I tell all. And more: I make stuff up, too. I don't mean for this to happen, but it does. Once I told all sorts of people that Don and Amy Brody were getting a divorce, that Don had a fellowship at Dartmouth and was taking the kids with him; and Amy was going to Salt Lake City. I said John Harris had told me this. I had an absolutely clear memory of John Harris giving me this scoop on his front porch. In my memory we were drinking sangria: which I think means blood, maybe in Spanish? a blood-red wine drink: I can still taste it, the blood-drink, the yummy flavor of the divorce story in my mouth.

It wasn't true.

It never happened. It absolutely never happened.

It must have been a dream; what else could it have been?

*

Vange's dream didn't come true either: that was maybe twenty years ago, and Randy is still going strong. Or as strong as he ever went.

None of us at the time could see what Annette saw in that guy.

He's got a good body though, Vange. You have to give him that.

I guess, said Vange.

Well, hell, Vange can't see much, what can you expect from her? Along these lines?

And it seems to me that you have to give Vange credit for coming right out with her prophecy, laying it on the line, so to speak.

Most of the old-time prophets, Nostradamus, guys like that, they didn't exactly predict *clearly,* you know. I mean. Have you ever, e.g., actually *read* Nostradamus? I have, and for all the clarity you get out of him, old N. might have been speaking in tongues.

I tried prophecy myself once, you know. I've tried just about everything in my life: the works: automatic writing, past-life regression (was that a trip?!), hypnosis. I'm a seeker, what they call a seeker in the occult racket. Not that there's anything occult about it any more; meaning hidden; it's all right out front now. Some things I tried were hard, and I never did manage them: out-of-body travel, for example. I never got the hang of it. Levitation.

But prophecy was easy. I just opened my mouth and out it came: *Part of the secret is in the ocean...part is in China....*

Well. Folks. My god. Part of the secret is probably in Flint, Michigan.

Speaking in tongues was easy too.

But what I'm getting at is that you have to admire Vange for not hedging her bets: she didn't say: *The jackal will eat the lotus, and stones be turned into banjos;* and you had to *figure out* from that that Randy would have a heart attack. No, folks: she came right out with it.

Dear old Vange.

*

Anyway. Back to my story. In the days when Yuri Geller first hit the papers: when he was, remember, doing things like bending forks with his mind?—a useful skill, that: a bent fork being what everybody needs.

But the point is, Vange was fascinated with Yuri Geller. She used to watch all the news programs so she could catch the latest on what Yuri was up to.

"Watch." You noticed that? Being blind--partially sighted, actually--she mainly just listened to the news. They used to have-- I guess they still have--a special TV set for blind people, with no picture, just sound. It was smaller than a regular TV, because of course it didn't need a picture tube; actually, it was about the size and shape of a VCR.

Vange had one of these in her office at the agency, plus a Talking Book Radio, and almost always when I went in there, one of them, the radio or the pictureless TV, would be playing. I don't know how she managed to get any work done at all. Well. Some people said she didn't, you know. Greg, the rehab director, was always mad at her.

I go in there and she's *listening to the radio!* Greg would say.

Or even: I go in there and she is *sleeping!*

Greg. I said. Many times. Have you ever asked Vange to do something and she didn't get it done? And better than anybody else could do it?

That's not the point, said Greg, obviously fuming, obviously furious. She should *look* like she's working!

Why? I said.

I thought he was going to hit me. I know he wanted to. *Because that's the way the world is set up!* he screamed. *You're supposed to look like you're working!*

The world isn't under my supervision, Gregory, I said. Vange is. Vange gets everything done that she's supposed to. And a lot more that nobody ever hears about....

I think she does it with mirrors, I said. I think she does it by magic.

Well, that made old Greg even crazier, of course. Greg was a newly-converted born-again, and the word "magic" was like a red flag to him. Why, he even made us give up our egg-hunt in the rehab center, that we had every year around Easter for the blind clients; he said that Easter eggs were pagan.

So: no magic for born-agains, that's for sure. Like John Wayne said in one of his movies: That's for dang sure.

*

No magic for the United Way either. The United Way was always trying to get Vange fired. As long as I was there, she was safe; I protected her; but after I left, she didn't last more than another year, year and a half, something like that.

*

Magic. Maybe that's what I should have called the story.

*

Story? I can hear you saying it: Is this a *story?* Where's the plot? When is something going to *happen?*

Well, I told you up front that I didn't have much: only a title: "Prophecy." Which should have been "The Prophet." Or "Magic." Maybe. I guess we'll have to wait and see how it all turns out.

But there'll be a story here eventually. You'll see. Trust me. It will be like a rabbit out of a hat. Zip! All of a sudden the story is going to be here: pop! And there you'll be, flat on your ass, holding a magic rabbit: you'll see.

Hang in.

What else is a story but magic?

Something out of nothing: that's a story. Or a picture. A piece of music. A poem. A dance. Gossamer. Sleight-of-hand: as they call it. Now you see it, now you don't. Now you see it. Now you see. Now.

It's like the TV for blind folks. It's magic makes the picture. Well. It's magic makes the sound too, isn't it? Think about it.

I had a friend once in college named Diedra. Diedra said that the world was full of magic, but we just didn't call it magic any more. Like a car key. A car key is twentieth century magic, she said. You stick the key in the car door and the door opens! Abracadabra! Alacazam! (Or however you spell that....)

Open sesame.

A car: a magic carpet. What's the difference? *Maybe the car only works because you think it will.*

Prove to me that I am wrong.

Maybe a key only opens a car door *today.* Maybe tomorrow it won't. How do you know? Yeah, but *how do you know?*

"When I was a child, I thought as a child. Now I am an adult, and I think as an adult...." *Why, you poor thing....I'm so sorry for you....*

Anyway. Yuri Geller. And Vange. Vange sat in her little office in the cross-corridor of the rehab center day after day, listening to the news about Yuri. And getting her work done by magic. Sleeping. Driving Gregory nuts.

And she would try to do what Yuri could do. She didn't ever like to know that anybody was better at stuff than she was--not even Yuri.

She never bent a fork: that I know of. And believe me: I would have known. She would have produced that bent fork in a second.

She wouldn't cheat, though: Vange. She wouldn't, like, bend a fork by some other means and produce it. No. Vange lies as much as the rest of us do, which is plenty, but about this stuff, her psychic powers and all, she wouldn't lie.

She did say one day that she had moved a cigarette pack with her mind.

The pack right there, she said. Pointing to a half-empty pack of Chesterfield Kings on her desk. Unfiltered. Vange at that time smoked—she has cut back now, but then she smoked—four packs of unfiltered Chesterfields a day; the hands that did her magic were badly stained; teeth too; and her desk and her person were always littered with ash and bits of tobacco. She was not a neat smoker. In fact, sometimes I could sort of see Greg's point: which was of course that Vange ought to clean up her act.

Greg himself was incredibly neat and tidy, his desk was always ship-shape. But as a matter of fact, it was Annette that made it that way, she came in at 7:30 every morning and cleaned off Greg's desk, dusted and put everything into piles and filed the piles in drawers.

You can manage to be neat quite easily when you a) have a good secretary, and b) don't do any real work worth mentioning.

But. Back to the cigarettes on Vange's desk.

I moved that pack of cigarettes by concentrating on it, she said. Just before you came in....

Wow, great, Vange, I said. How far?

(Well, it's a natural question. Isn't it? I mean, wouldn't you want to know?)

At least six inches, she said.

Wow, I said.

Well, see, I really believed in Vange. It really did impress the hell out of me that I could, for example, give her an assignment—not paperwork, our Vange was never high on paperwork, she could do it but she hated it—but, like, say, finding a suitable living arrangement for one of our out-of-town rehab center clients. She would dilly and dally and not do it and I would get more and more nervous as time went by; Vange, I would say, we only have four days left....

Plenty of time, she would say.

Trust me, she would say.

I wanted to, you know. And I did trust her, truly. But I got nervous anyway. Deep down, when I first began at the center, I was probably more like Gregory than I was like Vange. I learned, though, over my ten years there: to be more and more comfortable with it: I learned that there was no important advantage in being like Gregory.

All you could achieve being like Gregory was to impress the United Way and to make more money than the rest of us.

Not enough reward there, if you really looked at the thing.

And the rewards of being like Vange were clearly enormous. For openers, everybody—well, except for Greg and the U.W.— everybody loved Vange.

And even Greg, in his secret heart, I think, loved her. And-- God knows--depended on her for advice and last-minute miracles.

The living arrangement I had asked her to find, for example, would turn up, maybe a couple of days before the blind client was due to arrive.

It's at 1340 Fourth, Vange would say: I haven't seen it yet, do you want to drive me over there?

And I would drive her to see the apartment--listen folks, I'd do anything to get out of the office, and besides, I would really want to see what she had come up with. I mean, I really and truly believed that Vange could do miracles, but every now and then I needed a little reassurance. Every now and then I needed to see a little bitty miracle being pulled off.

And the place would be perfect. It would have, for example, a plump, grandmotherly landlady who happened to be a diabetic herself, so that she would a) understand the diabetic diet, and b) know what to do in case of an insulin reaction and c) be able to load insulin syringes.

All this for a terrified newly blinded young diabetic client.

My god, Vange, I would say. How did you get on to it?

Smirk. Nobody smirks like Vange.

Well. Except maybe Maeve, who I think might possibly come in here later.

Oh, well, you know....

I don't know, I say.

How did you fucking *do it?*

Well... one of my former clients came in yesterday...and he happened to know this man...who happened to....

The point is how did you *know that,* Vange? How did you *know that would happen?*

Ssmirk, smirk.

A pleased smirk was all I ever got by way of explanation. And a wave of that airy and delicate nicotine-stained hand.

But it never failed. It always worked for her. Whatever she did, magic or whatever, always worked.

*

However, I never saw her move the cigarette package.

How come I can't see you moving it, Vange? I said. How come you can't do it when I'm here?

Oh...well...I don't know...it takes so much concentration to do it... you distract me....

Your vibrations get in the way of mine....

Unsatisfactory.

I did believe, though. I absolutely did. But I am like Doubting Thomas, I want to stick my hand in.

I just want a little--uh, yeah, *proof.*

*

I mentioned Maeve a little while ago. I had another friend in those years, named Maeve--besides Vange, I mean, another friend besides Vange. I considered Vange to be a good friend even though at the Center I was technically her boss--I can hear you laughing, well, god, everybody else laughed at that idea too, and I have to laugh myself--anyway, for the whole ten years I was there Maeve had to hear all about my job and what went on at the Center and Greg and Annette and Randy and Vange and the egg hunt and all.

Vange was my work friend, those days, and Maeve was my weaving friend. Maeve and I would get together every Tuesday evening at her house to weave on portable wooden looms, maybe twenty inches square. Flat, and held across your lap. Our lap. Laps.

Maeve was a wonderful weaver. I wasn't as good as she was, but I was nevertheless, if I say so myself, quite good. I didn't stick to it, though--well, and I never stick to anything.

Writing, says Vange. You've stuck to writing your stories.

Well, yeah, that. Okay. But nothing else. I wouldn't even have stayed at the agency if Vange hadn't talked me into it. I mean, I had another job offer when I had been there exactly four months, and I didn't take it.

From Minneapolis Rehab: MRC as it was called then. Maybe still.

You don't want to work for MRC, said Vange. You'd hate it there.

Besides, she said. My experience is that you can't really even begin to know an agency until you've been there *at least* ten years....

And me, she said. Where else could you find me?

Well, I couldn't argue with that.

So I stayed. For ten years. Three months short of ten years. I'm leaving now, Greg, I said when I left: so I don't have to take the goddamn ten-year pin from you.

And Greg laughed. He always pretended that everything I said was a joke. No joke, folks.

*

Maeve was pretty interested in the psychic stuff I told her about Vange. Fascinated, actually.

And what do you know, now I've got two characters: Vange and Maeve. Three if you count Greg, which I personally never did.

And me. Four with me. Or three if you're not counting Gregory.

*

They put old Diedra in the bin after a while: remember her, the car-key magic person? It just goes to show you, doesn't it?—this magic stuff can be dangerous. Maybe silly old Greg was onto something when he banned Easter eggs?

I remember, though, that the clients loved the annual Easter egg hunt. I remember, for example, old Doc Rodriguez the last year we had the hunt. Doc was a dentist, and the oldest client we ever had in the RC. He was eighty-eight, and totally blind from ret. pig.--that's retinitis pigmentosa, but we called it ret. pig. Doc got down on his hands and knees to look for the eggs—he had this idea that we might have hidden them in the folds of the floor length curtain that masked the big window of the homemaking area.

Well. As Doc crawled around the RC floor I moved an egg so it was right in front of him. And--wouldn't you know it?—at the very last second, he veered. Missed the goddamn egg. Over and over again this happened: this *veering* at the last second. Well, I kept cracking up, of course I did, and everybody else did too, I mean there we all were, absolutely rolling around on the floor like lunatics, absolutely going to pieces: ho-ho-HO!

Even those clients who could see enough.

Doc: What's the matter with you, Joan? What's the matter with all of you?

Me: Oh, god, Doc...gasp, shout, hiccup.

Me: Oh, Doc, you don't *know*....

Fortunately Doc was a very tolerant person. And the story came out all right. Doc did finally bump into an egg. With his nose, if you can believe it.

*

Fairly early in my stay at the Center, Vange and I got onto the idea of changing people. It was quite simple, actually. We would just send good thoughts at someone, love thoughts, and they would change, just like that.

We called it Indirect Supportive Counseling when we wrote our reports for the state.

Honest to god. I am not making this up.

We did it the first time on a bus going home. Vange and I lived fairly near to each other, so we often took the same bus home. I could have driven, of course, but why? The bus was at least as reliable as my car and much more interesting.

Anyway, on this one day, the driver was this guy we called "Old Grumpy." Well: Vange called him Old Grumpy, *I* never called anybody Old Grumpy in my entire life: Horseshit Sonofabitch was more my style.

O.G. was even more G. than usual that day. He was being really rotten to the people who got on the bus. At one point he actually threatened, more or less, to run over somebody the next time he picked them up if they didn't stand back from the curb.

I mean, that might *happen,* yes, sure, but you don't have to threaten people ahead of time, do you?

Warn, yes. Not threaten.

I wonder who bent his finger back? I said to Vange.

Must have eaten tacks in his breakfast cereal, V. said.

And then: Let's think good thoughts at him, she said. Love thoughts. See what happens.

Okay, I said. And so we did.

Concentrating. As hard as we could. Staring at O.G.'s back as he drove the bus, smiling, goodness knows what we looked like, some kind of grinning Bobbsey Twins, maybe, sending love, love, *lo-o-o-ove.* Bombarding him: with sweetness. With acceptance. Affection.

Gregory would have been proud of us.

No, I guess he wouldn't, on second thought. Greg, if he'd have thought of it at all, and if he'd been on the bus, which of course he wouldn't be, not ever, Greg would have prayed for O.G. And prayer is okay too, you know; in fact, as far as I'm concerned it's the same thing; Vange and I just weren't into prayer on that particular day, that's all.

Well. In about ten minutes—less—Old Grumpy was laughing and smiling to beat the band. Once, he actually got off the bus to help an old lady get on.

Vange and I looked at each other and smiled. Smirked. Now I knew what the smirk was all about. Self-satisfaction?—oh, yeah. And how. You bet.

*

About that time was when me and Maeve started weaving. Weaving, you know, is magic too, in a way. Can be. Weaving can be like casting a spell, or like getting into a spell.

I am, for example, convinced that I got myself somehow or other into a real trance state when I was weaving once: about eight hours went by, I was alone in my house that day, and I simply wasn't conscious of any time passing at all.

Back...and forth....

On the little loom.

Again. Again. Again.

Careful. Careful. Get the sides...perfectly straight. Get...the...pattern...right....

Over and over: and my thoughts were back and forth too, and over and over. Patterns began to develop in my mind. I thought I could...see...things...understand...things....

When I realized what time it was, and how many hours had gone by, I was absolutely amazed.

Pleased, though, too; in a funny sort of way.

It did feel like a good thing to have been doing.

You know: this is strange: what it felt like was *prayer*. It felt like prayer.

*

The incident on the bus led me and Vange to think that we might be able to modify Greg too. I mean, Greg was not fun to be around at that time. Greg was making everybody's life miserable with his born-again stuff.

Vange thought up the procedure.

Since it's Gregory Roger we're talking about, she said--she knew Greg's full name because she had been at the agency when he first came, as a humble assistant and just off an Iowa farm-- since it's Gregory Roger we'll use prayer. Said Vange.

Okay with me, I said.

We'll meet every afternoon at four in the first-aid room and we'll pray for him. She said.

And that's what we did, folks. For maybe a month. We held hands, Vange and I, so that we made a circle, sort of, just the two of us, *where two or three are gathered,* like that, and we prayed.

God, please help Gregory Roger to like himself....

Dear Lord, please help Greg to feel more relaxed, less threatened....

Help us to see You in him....

Help us to love him....

And we'd send, every day, a magic circle, each of us our own kind, mine went around him, about hip level, with sparkles coming from it, like an electric hula hoop, or a fat inner tube made of light.

Vange's circle was more like a big egg shape—as I understood it—that the whole person fitted inside. But it had sparkles too, just like mine did.

Folks. We were entirely sincere about this. It was not a joke. Though I can just about hear you snickering in your beer out there, guys.

But you have to remember what it says in the Bible that people think so much of—the bedrock of our civilization, whether you like it or not: it said, *unless ye become as little children....*

Well. What do you think that *means?* It means what it says, that's what I think.

Well, anyway, our prayers worked. Right away, the first day. Greg started to mellow out a little, and after a while he would, for example, maybe thank Annette for the great job she did.

He told me how glad he was that I had come to the agency.

He told Vange how nice she looked—well, she did look good that day, but the point is he *told her.*

Good feelings were absolutely *rife.*

For about three weeks.

I mean, for three weeks we had paradise on earth, paradise in the rehab center.

Then, of all things, I got an attack of conscience.

I know this sounds screwy—even screwier than the foregoing, I mean--but you are just going to have to accept it. This is the way I am. I think it may be the result of being brought up as a Catholic: everything that seems to be any fun I eventually think is wrong.

We shouldn't be doing this, Vange, I said. There's something wrong with us doing this.

What can be wrong with it? said Vange.

Well, I don't know...maybe we should have, like *asked him* if it was okay to pray for him...maybe it's wrong to pray for somebody without asking their permission....

And: Maybe it's wrong to, like, try to interfere in the, you know, *cosmic plan?*

Also: Maybe the whole point of being able to do something like this is not to do it....

Etc., etc.

Vange said: I think you're supposed to use power if you've got it. For good...I think that's why you have it....

Me: But how do we know what's good?

Etc., etc.

Oh, you can go round and round on this one. But you get the idea.

Well, I think you're mistaken, said Vange. But if you really feel that way, obviously we can't do it any more.

So we stopped doing it. And life in the rehab center went back to normal: a little piece of hell. Well: maybe not that bad, but close enough.

I have to say this, though: Vange never held it against me. I know she thought I was a fool, but she didn't like me any less.

*

As I said before, my other friend Maeve was always interested in hearing about such stuff. Once her sister Emma in Portland had what seemed to be a poltergeist; and Maeve and I were all set to hop a bus to Portland to actually see this: but before we could do it, it turned out to be a squirrel.

Saved! said Maeve, laughing. Maeve's laugh is like little sticks breaking: *crack, crack, crack.*

I don't like travel anyway, she said.

Me neither, said I.

So, anyway, Maeve had to hear all about praying over Greg, and the cigarette package moving and all.

Do you think Vange could do table-turning? she asked one day.

I don't know, I said. I sat in Maeve's living room and ran my shuttle back and forth across the warp on my loom.

Maybe, I said.

Back—and forth. *Back*—and forth. Again and again.

Why not, I said. I'll ask her.

*

Table-turning? said Vange. Well, maybe. Well, sure. Why not? I don't know why not....

Hm. She said.

You and me and Maeve? She said. I should think we'd need at least three....

Great, I said. I'll tell Maeve.

And that way Vange would get to meet Maeve, too, or vice versa, which is probably more to the point: a consummation which I had been wishing for years.

*

One afternoon we assembled, me and Maeve and Vange, in my living room. Before they came I had cleared off the dining table: you have to have a table, obviously.

But Vange said it wouldn't do.

Nope, she said.

Too big. She said.

Too heavy.

There was a little round wicker table holding up a lamp in one corner of the room: that one, said Vange.

So I took the lamp off that table, ditto the covering cloth, and placed the table pretty much in the middle of the room. Then we got three straight dining room chairs and arranged them around the table. Sat.

Okay, said Vange. Now we need to get in tune with each other.

She held out her hands, one to each of us, and we took them, and took each other's hands too, and sat there feeling totally stupid, at least I did, but pretty interested anyway. Well, you have to understand that magic is counter-cultural—sitting around a little wicker table expecting the damn thing to move goes against every red-blooded American tenet. Magic is un-American. We have absolutely ruled out magic. Prayer too, lately: we're getting worse.

Feel the power? Said Vange.

Yeah, I said.

Uh-huh, said Maeve. Laughed.

Crack, crack, crack: little twigs snapping.

Actually, I didn't feel anything much then. At some other times I have felt something—maybe like a power surge—but not then.

But: Yeah, I said. I do feel it.

*

Anyway. On and on.

Close your eyes, says Vange.

Vange's hand is warm in mine: I would trust that hand to hold me back from a burning pit, but could it turn a table?

It's moving, says V.

Feel that?

Uh—yeah....

I say.

I open my eyes just a crack.

Keep your eyes closed, says Vange.

Snap. Shut. Wow.

But. I choose two markers while my eyes are open: a particular rib on the wicker surface of the table and the flue handle on the fireplace were exactly in line. How's that for faith? How's that for confidence?

Let's hear it for skepticism.

*

When it was all over, we stood up and stretched ourselves, shook ourselves out, like rugs too long rolled up. This concentration is terrifically hard work.

*

Then: It moved, said Vange. Did you feel it move?

Yeah, I said. I did feel it. I think I did.

Just a little, said Vange. Not a lot. You can't expect a lot the first time....

Well. Hm. The three of us chatted for a little while. Then: Want a ride home, Vange?

I said.

Okay, said Vange.

*

On the way to Maeve's house--I took Vange home first, it was right on the way; neither Vange nor Maeve drives, Vange for obvious reasons and Maeve because she doesn't do anything mechanical, working a microwave is tough for her—on the way, Maeve said: It didn't move.

No it didn't, I said.

I took a bearing to make sure, she said. One of the wicker pieces on the table and your nose. She laughed: *crack, crack*. I stared at her.

You too, I said: I did that too. Took a bearing. But I used the flue knob on the fireplace. I said.

We looked at each other for a long moment. The car veered a little bit, and I corrected it. Then we began to laugh: *Ha-ha-ha! Crack-crack-crack*....

Not at Vange, though, you know. At something else.

*

Maeve and Vange never met again after that day, and I stopped trying to get them together. These things are more or less hopeless: they happen or they don't. They can't be made to work.

East is east. As they say.

I don't work at the Center for the Blind any more. Instead, I take care of people who have Alzheimer's disease now. I'm a free-lance—I got tired of having bosses, and now I don't have one.

I got a new client a few weeks ago. Her name is Suzanne. Suzanne lives in an apartment in Walker Place, which is a residence for older people. She is full of wisdom. She astonishes me sometimes. I listen carefully to her: I know now that God's messages can come from anyone.

People are the real miracles, she says.

How do you figure that, Suzanne? I say.

Because they can see, she says. They have these round things in their faces, and they can *see out of them*....

And they can *think*...they have brains in their heads and they can *think with them*....

Isn't that a miracle?

Even if they think funny, like I do. She says.

Oh, Suzanne....

I hug her. Suzanne, you're *so smart*, I say. She laughs. I know she is pleased.

Suzanne loves me and I love Suzanne.

*

Vange didn't make the table turn. She didn't bend a fork. But she bent *me*—she turned *me:* a little bit. Maybe the important thing is not that the prophets should be right, but that there should be prophecy. Maybe the prophets, whoever they are, Nostradamus or Vange or even me, maybe they carry a seed for all of us, maybe they carry a promise and a memory: that once there was magic on the earth and there can be magic again.

And in my heart I continue secretly to believe that when all things are right, when all the vibrations are perfect, Vange will bend a fork. She will turn a table.

She didn't foretell a heart attack for Randy, but she could. Sometime. For somebody.

Or something else. Maybe not a heart attack. Maybe something very, very good.

Me too. Some day *I* will.

Some day someone will open my held-back and divided heart to the doing of miracles, the speaking of prophecy. And the very same instant that I believe, it will all be true. That's my prophecy.

It can happen.

We can change.

YES, BUT WHAT ABOUT....

I

Anne Morgan?

Anne came into my office at the Minneapolis Center for the Blind one morning for a routine intake interview. I was an ACSW social worker—which signifies Academy of Certified Social Workers, and at that time it meant something: generally, that you were a real hotshot—which would certainly have qualified me for a high-level administrative position, but there I was, doing a lowly task like intake.

The truth is, I was the manager of Community Services, but I hung onto the intake function like a lifeline. It gave me the only direct contact I had with honest-to-god clients, students, patients, whatever, there was an ongoing argument about what to call these folks.

(Christ, could it matter...?)

Hello, Anne, I said. I sat behind my desk and she sat stiffly beside her rehabilitation counselor from SSB, State Services for the Blind, Ron Allison.

I'm Joan Shepherd. I said. I guess Ron has told you what I do here.

Hello, she said. He said you were a hotshot. The top of the line.

Well, what can you say?

He's right, I said. Laughed.

Do you think she cracked a smile? Hell, no. Her pretty young face was frozen into a tight mask. I knew from the case file that she was 24 years old and a juvenile diabetic, and blind because of the diabetes.

"Juvenile" didn't mean that you were a kid or anything, it meant that you had developed diabetes before you were, like *old*.

Did Ron explain to you what it is that we do here?

I said.

He said you'd teach me to function as an efficient blind person.

She said. Flat voice. Disbelief in every syllable.

That's right, I said. That's part of it.

What else could there be? she said.

Hostile, my God.

Usually I could break through hostility.

Not this time.

Anne was hard-core.

*

The thing is, I loved intake, and I was very, very good at it. I have my father's gift—I can charm people most of the time, I can make them like me, and when they like me, they believe what I say.

The clients I worked with at MCB, most of them, were newly blinded. Mostly diabetic. They came in believing that their lives were over, that they could never be okay again, never be happy again.

What I told them in essence was that they *could* be happy again, that I and all the rest of us—mobility instructors, who taught blind people to get around with the white cane; Braille teachers; abacus teachers for math (in those days we had abaci, not the talking calculators they have now; this interview took place maybe thirty years ago); teachers for what we called Activities of Daily Living, or ADL's: cleaning, cooking, hygiene, etc.

Craft instructors, who for example taught blind clients to work with power tools; and to do macramé: for another example.

Recreation specialists who taught them to ski. To canoe. Play baseball. Bowl.

(That blind ski team. That was something else. How it worked was that a sighted person—that's you and me, babe; so far—went down the hill with a blind person, side by side and holding hands.

(Once the King of Sweden came over to see what we did. We assigned our best skier, a kid named Richard Hillela, to ski with him. We were so excited, my God, *the King of Sweden,* I mean, in Minnesota, that's *big.*

(But at the last minute the king sent a substitute. Some lower level emissary. Richard skied with this guy, and something went wrong, and there was a huge end-over-end fall, the Swede and Richard, a mad rolling ball of arms and legs and red hats and skis.

(Big time embarrassment all around. Nobody, thank God, was seriously hurt. A few bangs and scrapes—nothing much.

(Think of it this way, Richard said. To me. Afterwards. It could have been the King of Sweden.

(We did learn to take our lumps in this business.)

But not Anne. No dice.

What do you—or did you—do for a living, Anne? I said, that first day in my office.

I'm a racecar driver, she said.

I looked at Ron, who was totally letting me carry the ball in this interview. I think he was as flummoxed by Anne as I was beginning to be.

He nodded. Yes. No joke.

Well, Christ. If she'd said she was a pilot, even that would have been better. You can fly blind these days with instruments.

I guess that's pretty much over, I said.

No it isn't, she said. I'll drive again. I'll see again. This is not permanent. This is not forever.

*

You have to understand here that there were "good" blind people and "bad" blind people.

As there were good quads and bad quads when I took my social work training at Kenny Rehab here in Minneapolis. A "good quad" pretty much accepted that he or—sometimes—she would never walk again, would never move much again below the neck. The amount of movement depended on the level of the injury—C6, for example, designated injury to the 6th cervical vertebra in the spine. The higher the injured vertebra, the less movement there would be. Ever.

The highest I ever worked with—a guy from Virginia, Minnesota—was a C7.

A "good quad" changed his expectations of what he could do, and mastered all the things we could teach him. Learned to feed himself, for example, with an adapted spoon fastened to his wrist. Learned to get around in a motorized wheel chair.

A bad quad more or less just sat there and said: No Way. I am going to get better, I am going to walk again.

Destroy his hope, the rehab docs would tell us. He will never learn to be as good as he could be as long as he believes there is hope....

But there was, with the quads, a middle ground, in which the guy—they mostly were guys, as it happened, who had been injured in sports accidents, or at least that was true forty years ago—accepted what we had to teach him, tried hard, worked hard, but regarded it all as a temporary fix, believed that someday something would be discovered that would let him walk again.

Personally, I always hated the directive: Kill Hope. I was a dissenter, a fifth-columnist. I had hope too. I believed in hope too. For them and for myself.

(And hey—nowadays there's, like, stem-cell research and all....)

*

Ditto blind people. Good and bad blind people. They accepted their situation or they didn't. Anne pretty much turned out to be a middle-grounder—she put her talents and her fine intelligence to work on the many tasks we could teach her, and—because she was so smart—she did okay. But it was like learning to knit in jail—you'd never believe you'd have much use for it after you got out. It would never become what you'd call a passion, or a way of life.

*

I saw all clients in my office at least once or twice in the course of their time with us—usually three or four months.

I asked Anne to come in to see me one day. She opened the door, tapped her way over to my desk with her cane, found a chair, sat.

Hey, Anne, I said.

Hello, Mrs. Shepherd, she said.

Call me Joan. Everybody does.

I said.

I am not that kind of informal person, Mrs. Shepherd, she said.

Oh…kay….

How's it going, I said.

All right, she said. I guess.

She was a very pretty girl, beautiful, maybe. Long straight black hair, shiny as coal, a classic face, beautifully-shaped mouth, nice nose. Black eyes that saw nothing. Or maybe light. Maybe shadows. Nothing useful. A diabetic from age seven.

She had a lithe, slender body. Average height.

Your teachers tell me you could be doing a lot better, I said.

Do they? she said. Not exactly insolent, but coming awfully close.

Yes, they do. I said.

Then she broke. I hate this, she said. I hate everything about this. I don't want to be blind. I *won't* be blind. *I refuse to be blind….*

*

Let this cup be taken from me….

*

When I told Anne that we did other stuff besides just teaching students to be competent blind people? Remember?

What I meant was that we worked with the whole person. We—for example—taught grumps how to have fun. Taught loners to love their neighbors. Brought shy, scared, timid folks out.

I remember one guy who had shot himself through the head in a failed suicide pact. Essentially he performed a partial frontal lobotomy and destroyed both optic nerves. The docs said: Forget it. He'll always be a vegetable. Before we got through with him he went to college, got a degree, married and fathered a child. He said to me: I'm glad I did it. I'm glad it happened. If I'd never been blind, I couldn't have come here, and my life is better now than it ever was before….

I worked with another guy who knew nothing but books; he was shy, alone, embittered. It wasn't so much the content of books as the actual books that fascinated him: beautiful bindings, beautiful paper, that he could never see again. I taught that guy to

151

substitute people, knowing about people, loving people, for books: and would you believe he ended up as a big shot in the Minnesota Senior Federation? No joke, he really did.

We thought we could do miracles. And we *did* do miracles—all the time. But we were baffled and stymied by Anne. Anne never bought into the premise—that there could be life after blindness—she never joined the community. She stayed outside and aloof.

*

I'm going to see again, Anne said that day in my office. Softly.

Well, what could I say? I hope you're right, Anne, I said.

Lame? Oh, yeah. Chicken? Oh, yeah.

What is it that you love so much about being a racecar driver, Anne? I asked.

I—I—can't tell you, she said. You—have to be there, you have to *do it* before you can understand....

Is it the speed? I said.

Yes, she said. You could say that. *It's the speed....*

So it wasn't the speed. Well, maybe it was partly the speed.

But maybe it was also the control over the machine you drove. Maybe it was the collaboration between you and the machine.

If it was that, I could relate to it. I learned to drive out in the country, on country roads. I have never liked driving in the city. But I did like driving on those bumpy, dirty, washboard gravel, what they called washboard, country roads, with a bandana over my nose and mouth to protect somewhat against the clouds of dust.

And best of all was driving in a blizzard. I *loved* driving in a snowstorm out in the country. It felt like me and the car were almost one entity, and between us we could defeat the storm, transcend human limits....

*

Can nothing replace it, Anne? Not skiing, for example? Nothing, she said.

Her face was adamant. Stone.

*

I think suddenly of a line from *Lawrence of Arabia,* when the general says to T. E. Lawrence: "It is a fearful thing to refuse one's destiny...."

*

But hey. I *did* hope. I hoped for *all* or them; I hoped for *me.* Didn't I? Didn't I have to? Don't *you* have to? Hope against hope. Hope that we can stop time, the march of death, disability, age. Hope that we can stop climate change. Hope that human beings can learn to live together in peace.
Yeah, right.
And on the other hand, *right.*
What else is there?

*

In my heart I admired the bad quads. And the bad blind people. And the Dems who voted for Al Gore. The ones who hoped.
My daughter sent me a button for Christmas that says: I'M IN. I GIVE A DAMN. It's my favorite Christmas present of all.
I am still broke from the money I dumped into Al Gore's campaign. Now you know where I stand. I'm a hoper.

*

And hey, we elected Barack Obama in 2008. That sure as hell took hope.

*

Blind diabetics did not get better. Diabetes, in those days, was a death sentence. The life expectancy of a juvenile diabetic—now they call it Type I—diagnosed in early childhood or adolescence usually—was about 35 years.
There is also a Type II diabetes that occurs later in life—Adult Onset, we called it then—and the prognosis for that was pretty dire too. The Type II's lived longer, but they went blind faster.
And hey—not just blind. There were other complications: for both groups. Renal failure; and dialysis and kidney transplant. Heart disease. Blood pressure problems: high and low. High blood pressure and low blood pressure. Neuropathy, sometimes in the fingers, but mostly in the legs and feet; pain and gangrene and amputation. Not all at once: no such luck. First a toe; doesn't

sound like much, but losing a toe disturbs your balance, big time.
Then the foot. Then the leg below the knee. Then at the thigh.
Well, you get the picture: Goya, maybe. His Christs on crosses.

I feel as though my body has become the enemy, a blind
diabetic said to me in my office once.

So you see, Anne didn't have much to look forward to.
Probably some kind of denial was her best bet.

*

At the Minneapolis Center for the Blind, I came to believe that
denial could be seen as the finest flower of the human mind.

*

One of the things you need to know about diabetics is that
some people believed that there was such a thing as a "diabetic
personality." Generally, the ones who believed it were those who
worked most closely with diabetics.

I believed it.

We all talked about it a lot: the staff at MCB.

Hey, Janet, do you think there is really a...etc.

Janet was an ADL's instructor. ADL's--I told you about that.
Activities of Daily Living.

Oh, absolutely, said Janet.

Take Anne.

Anne....

I said.

Anne is a perfect diabetic personality, Janet said.

She just goes through the motions here. I mean, she's good at
the stuff I can teach her, but she doesn't really care.

She totally hates it. She totally believes that life will not be
worth living if she stays blind. And if I tell her that there is a rule
about something, pairing socks, say, she defies it, she finds a
different way to do it....

Her way is okay, it'll work all right, but my way is tried and
true, mine is easier.

Anne doesn't do anything the easy way....

In fact, you know, Janet said, I could see her committing
suicide....

*

Most of the diabetics were very intelligent. Most of them were high achievers. Most of them were charming as hell. And far too many of them thrived on competition, and loved danger. I am as sure as I can be that there was, among the hundreds of diabetics I interviewed, a much higher percentage than you would find in the general population of: skiers, mountain climbers, motorcyclists, pilots, skydivers, champion skaters, champion swimmers, well, you get the idea.

Anne was the only car racer, and the only one that fought blindness as hard as she did. The others transferred their drive to overcoming blindness, became champion blind people. And listen, what could it matter, most of them died so young....

*

And, contrary to what the docs in those days would have told you, maybe would tell you even now, it wasn't only the ones who failed to take good care of themselves who died.

Jennifer Halverson, one of the nurses who set up the Diabetes Education Center at Nicollet Clinic—where I became a lecturer; I think my main function was to scare the shit out of newly diagnosed diabetics, representing as I did all the terrible things that *could happen*—anyway, Jennifer Halverson did absolutely everything she could to stay healthy; and the recommended diabetic regimen in those days was *hard,* sort of the equivalent of being asked to balance on one thumb for the rest of your life; Jennifer tried hard, but she died at the age of twenty-six nevertheless.

(I always thought that the diabetes docs wanted to blame their patients for not shaping up, because it saved them from having to say: We don't know. We *think* that if you do it this way, you'd have a better chance, but we *don't know.*

(I know a doc who, when I described a symptom and asked him what it was, said: Beats me. And I thought: This is a good doc; and I have hung in with him for thirty years now. I followed him to a clinic in Maplewood, which is a long, long way from where I live.)

*

I mentioned the charm factor? We all—the staff—loved the diabetics, fell for the diabetics, wept when they died. As so many of them did. I told you that the average life expectancy was 35 years?

Some of them beat the odds. Some of them lived—if you could call the life of a blind diabetic living, it looked like slow crucifixion to me—some of them lived for a lot of years.

No matter what the odds were, they all—almost all—believed that they would beat them. They believed what we all—almost all—believe, hope: that they would, could, somehow live forever.

Believing that they would live forever, they did what other folks did: they fell in love, they married, they had children.

And actually, several members of our staff married blind diabetics. One of the mobility instructors married an aide from the ADL area. Janet—the ADL instructor that I told you about, who said she thought Anne Morgan might kill herself—Janet married a perfectly delightful guy named John Stevenson. John was one of the ones who lived for many years beyond what he could have expected. He became a massage therapist, and he and Janet had a child: a little girl: Jocelyn, who was diagnosed diabetic when she was only a couple of months old.

I don't care, said Janet. I deserve to have a happy life. I never thought I would. I never thought I'd have a husband, I never thought I'd be a mother....

John died (I learned at an agency function recently; I go back now and then to attend teas when somebody I knew in the long-ago past retires) anyway, John died just a short while ago which means that he lived for maybe 60 or 65 years.

Janet talked about John's death with tears in her eyes.

Everybody told me not to marry John, she said. You told me not to, Joan (me—remember?) But I was never sorry that I did. We had a lot of happy years together. I truly believe that it was happiness that kept him alive that many years.

I was never sorry that I decided to marry him.

I didn't have the guts to ask about Jocelyn. Everybody told Janet not to have a child, too. The odds were at least 50% that a child of hers and John's would be diabetic.

We worked with a doctor as a consultant, George Bryant his name was, who was himself a diabetic; the gene for diabetes was, he said, so prevalent in this country that within 30 years diabetes would be epidemic. And look, folks: it's 30 years later now and we have an epidemic of diabetes on our hands. The doc was right.

It isn't just that people eat too much, or eat wrong, you know; you have to have the gene too. Both.

But hey! They are discovering so many new things to help control diabetes these days. Maybe Jocelyn will be okay.

There's always hope. Isn't there?

II

Well, no, not always.

Our darling secretary, Lynnie Clare—yes, that was really her name, first and last—married a guy we all loved: Kenneth Damon.

Kenneth was the first person ever in what became our diabetes program. The diabetes program was so good that it became actually famous all over the country: Barb Warren and I (Barb was the nurse with whom I set up the program) went to New York and Chicago and lots of other cities to tell them how we did it.

(Hey—*world*-famous, if you count the postcard we got from Moscow....)

When Kenny was referred, Barb had just started working with me. I had complained to a State Services counselor, Sherri Johnson, that I had to read all these medical reports on our clients and I just didn't understand them, I mean, I could look up the words but I didn't know what the conglomerate signified: what it meant in terms of what the client could do in our program, what arrangements, adaptations, we had to make.

Bitch, bitch—to Sherri.

Why don't you, she said, get a nurse to help you?

The agency can't afford a nurse, I said. Glum.

They can barely afford me.

Get a volunteer, she said. There must be some nurses among your list of volunteers....

Hey. Light bulb. Flash of lightning. Saul on the road to Damascus: *Get a volunteer.* Hey. Wow.

I talked to my volunteer coordinator, and sure enough, there was a nurse driving for the Birthday Club.

I remember the exact day, the exact time, place, I called her. The exact words I said.

A Sunday morning, in my kitchen in my house on Bryant Avenue, an old-fashioned black dial phone.

Hi, I said, when someone answered. May I speak to Barbara Warren?

This is Barb, she said.

Hey, I said, have I got a deal for you....

And that began it all—the years of joy and excitement and grief and major stress.

After that she came in to read and interpret the case files one morning a week: Tuesdays. She was my liaison with the docs: she could speak their language. And—as important—she could charm birds out of trees. The docs, eventually, ate out of her hand. Called her at home. Schmoozed with her. Cried with her.

She didn't stay volunteer and one-morning-a-week for long. Eventually, she was paid and worked three days a week—I could tell you how I managed that, but it's another story, and this one is getting long enough as it is.

*

So. Anyway. Kenny Damon.

One day—Tuesday morning, as it happened—Barb and I were sitting in my office and Stuart Jacobs, a counselor from Rochester—yeah, the Rochester of the Mayo Clinic—called.

I've got a kid here who is as brittle as they come. He said.

"Brittle"—in those days (maybe now too) we used the word "brittle" to describe a diabetic whose disease was unstable and unpredictable, whose blood sugar plunged up and down according to no laws that anyone understood. It was the fluctuation of the blood sugar that caused—anyway, that's what all the diabetes experts thought—all the complications: blindness, neuropathy, kidney failure.

His name is Kenny Damon. He's running 4+ most of the time. Said Stuart.

4+--I suppose you need to know what that means too. I suppose you need to know it all. But there was so much to know: Barbara and I truly were experts by the time we were done—for sheer willingness to study, master facts and interrelationships and the prognosis if this—this—this—happened—Barb and I, as I was saying, deserved all the acclaim we got.

George Bryant—you remember him, our diabetes consultant—said once that to know diabetes was to know the human body, because diabetes affected every system in the body:

brain, heart, nerves, kidneys, liver, periphery (hands and feet and legs) and colon (we had a woman once whose lower bowel was paralyzed because of neuropathy; Christ, can you imagine, she couldn't shit on her own, had to have big-time enemas every two or three weeks, and was incredibly uncomfortable in between; when she died, her doc said he didn't know why, there was no reason for her to actually *die*; and I thought: hey, wouldn't *you* give up about then, wouldn't *you* die? if you could manage it?

Frances, her name was. I went to her funeral at the temple on Hennepin.

*

4+ meant one step above death. It meant you could go into a diabetic coma and die. They didn't get a lot worse than that.

He has to have special meals, Stuart said. Here in Rochester he eats in the hospital cafeteria.

My god, I said. I don't know that we are equipped to handle that. Meals at a *hospital?* I don't know, Stuart.

At least meet the kid, he said. Everybody falls in love with him. Everybody.

I turned away from the phone. Barb, I said. You talk to Stuart. This is way out of my league.

So Barb talked to Stuart. Finally: Send the case file, she said. We can look at it. *Making no promises, you understand….*

When she got off the phone: Can we do it? I said.

If anybody can, we can, she said. Her black eyes—set in a head so smart, so gifted, so full of humor and daring—sparkled.

And that was the start of the world-famous diabetes program.

Lord, we had fun. Sometimes I miss those years—the excitement, the challenge, the joy, the tears. The few times we had to say—very few times, in fact at this moment I can't remember one—the times we had to say: We can't.

*

At first we set up Kenny's meals at old Eitel Hospital and sent him over there in a cab three times a day. We found him a room in a boarding house that we used pretty often, where the manager—Betty—was herself a diabetic and so understood the problems. A great human being, old Betty, a huge help to us in our World-Famous Program.

Barb measured out Kenny's insulin in a whole lot of syringes, a week's-worth at a time, and Betty kept them in the fridge at the boarding house. She or Barb gave him his shots—three or four a day, I seem to remember—until we taught him to do it himself. And eventually we taught him to measure his own insulin, using an instrument called an Insulgage.

Old-fashioned now, I'd guess, but then it was a life-saver. It was made by a PhD. psychologist in Denver, Colorado, in his basement workshop. Each insulgage was made individually, by hand, by this guy. I wish I could remember his name, I'd like to give him the credit he deserves. Hey, I'll ask Barb; maybe she remembers. I'll ask her when she gets back from Arizona, where she winters now with her husband, Richard; she can do that now that she has retired from her job at MCB.

Before she retired, she was a) full time, b) a board member, c) the manager of the Rehab Center, and d) the executive director of the whole shebang.

(Hey, have I got a deal for you....)

(You absolutely never can tell what is going to happen, can you? You absolutely never know, do you? what the next day will bring, what is around the next corner....)

*

The thing was, Barb couldn't stand it that such a little thing as not being able to measure their own insulin stood between the blind diabetics and the independence they so wanted.

You can understand how much they would want it when you remember The Diabetic Personality.

So Barb got hold of this guy, the psychologist, on some rehab grapevine and convinced him to keep working on his invention, and eventually to make it for us individually, for individual clients. He came to Minnesota to teach us to use it; and he taught us both, her and me, one of us under a blindfold, to teach our blind clients to use it. I have to admit that I was never altogether comfortable teaching it—I mean, we were talking life-and-death here.

His other claim to fame—this wonderful PhD. psychologist from Colorado—was that he was born with six or seven livers. Honest to God, I am not making this up.

*

After a while we had Kenny measuring and administering his own insulin. And he became stable enough so that he only had to have supper at Eitel—breakfast and lunch were planned out by Barb and the Eitel dietician and prepared by Betty at the boarding house; he carried his lunch in a brown bag to the agency; and so to that extent he was, and felt himself to be, like our other students. Not quite so far out of the norm.

And he was happy and cheerful and sunny all the time. Stuart—remember old Stuart, the counselor from Rochester?—was right: we all fell in love with him. Everybody fell in love with him.

Including our secretary, little Lynnie Clare.

*

His doctor in Rochester—Kenny went back for an examination maybe once a month—his doctor called us and said: What the hell are you guys doing? He ran 4+ consistently down here and now he's running 1+ and 2+. *What are you doing?*

He's happy here, I told the doc. We are making him happy....

Barb asked Kenny at some point, maybe in the intake interview, which she sat in on with me: Are there things you wanted to do in your life that you can't do now?

He named off a few things: the usual: climb Mount Everest, go on safari in Africa....

But one of the things he wanted to do was smaller, maybe manageable.

He wanted to go on a canoe trip.

Well. Barbara and Richard were big into the outdoors. They did a lot of canoeing in the northern part of the state, which, if you have forgotten, is Minnesota.

I think maybe we could pull it off....

She said.

To me. One day.

Said nothing to Kenny, of course, until she had it all arranged.

She lined up a doc at Nicollet Clinic—Doctor Meyers, a honey if there ever was one—who understood our philosophy ("Make 'Em Happy") and agreed to be on standby while Barb and Richard took Kenny for a weekend on the St. Croix River. Not so far away that they couldn't get to a medical facility fairly quickly; and not so near that it was clearly a sham.

She got a dietician at Eitel to help set up food for the few days they'd be gone. She actually talked a butcher into making some salt-free hotdogs, can you imagine?

And they did it—hot damn!—they took Kenny on a canoe trip.

Did he enjoy it? I asked her. Later.

Did he love it?

Oh, absolutely, she said.

He was quiet about it, but happiness just shone out of his eyes....

She said.

Did he help paddle?

He did, she said. He totally pulled his weight. He helped set up the camp, helped carry stuff, he was fine.

*

Lynnie Clare: she was the dearest, sweetest, prettiest thing. And one of the best secretaries I ever had. She was twenty years old: a baby. We began to notice Kenny hanging around Lynnie's desk whenever he had a free moment, and we all said: Uh-huh....

Some of us, the social workers, me and Vange, said: Oh-oh.

(There's a difference between uh-huh and oh-oh—the difference is trepidation. The difference is fear.)

Vange—I have to introduce you to Vange now. Vange Kuhlman was the best social worker I ever knew. When I first came to the agency she was about fifty years old, fat and blind, and not in good shape. Her husband—sighted—had died about a year before, and she just wasn't getting over the loss.

The first day I was there, Ray Armstrong, the guy who hired me (he hired me on the basis of one question: Could you tell a blind man his fly was open? I could if it was, I said; and I was in) Ray said: Your first job is to fire Vange.

You can tell a lot about the agency's management style just from that, can't you?

Well, I thought it over for three days of fear and trembling; after all, this was my first real job, and I was lucky to have it; the job market for social workers was very tight (Richard Nixon, he who blamed all the troubles of the whole country on the social workers, had just got in during my second year in the School of

Social Work at the University of Minnesota); I was a single mom trying to support an eight-year-old daughter; well, you get the idea. I was scared shitless.

After three days I came back to Ray—listen, I give myself full marks for this, it was a very hard thing to do—and said: Ray, I won't fire somebody that I don't know. Give me six months. I believe that I can do miracles. If I can't shape Vange Kuhlman up in six months, I'll fire her, and you can fire me.

Well, hey, wow. In six months Vange was a huge asset to the agency, and to me. She's the one who found the wonderful boarding house that we used for Kenny Damon. For example. She organized the United Way picnic that year so successfully that more people from more agencies came than ever came before in the whole history of the event.

And Vange was the person people went to when they had trouble.

Kenny came to her one day.

Lynnie and I are in love, he said. We want to get married.

He raised his hand before she could speak: I know this because she told me afterward: Don't say anything, he said.

I know how crazy it is, he said.

I know what the odds are.

I try to tell her, but she won't listen to me. She won't listen, she can't hear....

Kenny sat in Vange's office and held his head in his hands.

I'm going to marry her, he said, muffled. I love her so much. She loves me so much. She wants us to be married.

I want it too....

A child...said Vange.

I swear to you there will be no child....

Then, if you've made up your minds, what can I do?

Said Vange.

Talk to her, Kenny said. I can't marry her if I don't do what I can to make sure she knows ahead of time what's going to happen....

She'll hate me for it, Vange said.

I know, said Kenny. I know I'm asking a lot. I know what I'm asking.

Will you do it?

Well, she didn't promise right away. I'll give her that. How could she? She so totally disapproved of the whole thing. She thought about it. She talked it over with me.

But eventually: I'll talk to her, she told Kenny.

Better you than me, I said. You'll know how to be kind....

There is no way to do this and be kind, she said, her face set into a mask.

*

She called Lynnie in to her office. The interview took about fifteen minutes. Then Lynnie stormed out, dashed to the coat-closet, grabbed her coat and ran out, shrugging into the coat as she ran.

She came back the next day, as sunny and sweet as ever. But she never spoke to Vange again, except when it was necessary for her job.

Kenny spoke to Vange once: Thanks, he said.

*

Lynnie and Kenneth were married in a small, quiet ceremony. No one from the agency was invited except one secretary, who was Lynnie's special friend. Apart from that friend, only Lynnie's parents, and Kenny's up from Rochester, attended.

Lynnie left the agency soon after the wedding.

We heard that the two of them lived together in a small apartment for about two years before Kenny died. God only knows what went on before that death.

Maybe it was merciful. Maybe it was sudden.

Kenny was as good as his word: there was no child.

*

Vange told me that she met Lynnie on the street once after that.

She talked to me, Vange said, tears streaming down her fat old face, blurring her blind eyes.

She thanked me for what I tried to do....

She said she understood now....

*

As far as I ever heard, Lynnie never married again. How could she? After that? Still. You don't know, do you? You absolutely never know. You can always hope.

III

One day, a couple of years later, we heard some extraordinary news about Anne Morgan. We heard that she had gotten her sight back, and was driving racecars again.

How can that be? we said. You say.

I don't know, but it was true. It did happen.

Vange said it was a miracle.

I thought that Anne had so firmly set her mind against being blind that she—somehow—made it happen.

In any dire situation after that, in any apparently hopeless situation, somebody would always say: Yes, but what about Anne Morgan? It became a watchword at the agency. It became a watchword in my life.

Greenland is melting? Human beings are busy destroying their planet? Well, yes.

Yes.

But what about...?

THE SAMARITAN

Me and Vange were into magic. You probably know that already if you've read my other stories—and why wouldn't you? They are all good stories.

We rode the bus together every afternoon after work—maybe at 5pm, 5:15. The #4 bus going south from Franklin. Vange always got off on 38th Street and I got off eight blocks later. You don't need to know this, but what the hell.

Anyway. For lack of anything better to do, and to bring ourselves back to a decent frame of mind after a rough day at the agency—the Minneapolis Center for the Blind, and all the days were rough—sometimes we did a little magic. Just for fun.

There was one driver that Vange called Old Grumpy. He was a sour old guy, maybe 50 or 55, bald as an egg, no fringe, nothing. He had a terrible cough and he hacked and hawked into a handkerchief. He never had a good word for anybody. He looked a lot like what I imagine Ichabod Crane might have looked like. Well, except for the hair, I think I.C. had long lank brown hair.

People asked this driver questions—this is an example of how mean he could be—about how to get where they were going and sometimes he gave them wrong information. We thought he did it on purpose. I mean, what would make a real curmudgeon happier than thinking about some poor soul stranded on 142nd and Penn without a clue?

Vange and I would—after the driver gave wrong directions— set the person straight, give him or her the right dope.

(Don't do what he says, dearie. Get off on Lake Street and take the 21 going East, and then catch the #18 going south. That will get you there. Here—here's a schedule. The 21 runs real often, and so does the 18....)

The driver would glare at us.

Ruining his misanthropic fun *again.*

Vange and I were bus people as surely as that driver was. Neither of us drove a car—Vange because she was legally blind, and me by choice. I was, like, saving the planet, long before Al Gore made it the in thing. Speaking of Al Gore, you may not know this, but we really *need* old Al. By and large, people have to be helped to be good, forced if you will—to even see what good is.

One day that bus driver was even crabbier than usual. We speculated—as always—on the cause; we made up stories.

Maybe his wife packed him an egg-salad sandwich, and eggs don't agree with him.

Said Vange.

Maybe he has dyspepsia.

Maybe someone reported him to his supervisor.

Maybe he caught hell this morning.

That was my contribution.

Suddenly: out of the blue: Let's think good thoughts at him, said Vange. We looked at each other. Oh, wow. This could be fun. So from about 24th and Lyndale, we sat and thought good thoughts at Old Grumpy: just sent him wave after wave of kindness and love.

Hey, babe, it worked a treat.

In just a few blocks he was saying Hello to people when they got on. He was smiling like anything. At Lake Street an old lady tried to wrestle a big cart onto the bus and she was having a hell of a time. That crabby driver actually *got off the bus* and helped her on first and then lifted the cart on and settled it in front of her on one of the long side seats.

Vange and I looked at each other. Wow, I said. Wow, Vange.

Honestly, this really did happen. I am totally not making this up. But we were both pretty amazed at how fast this had worked, and how thoroughly. I mean, we'd done magic before. And we got some pretty spectacular results sometimes, but this was amazing. This was way over the top.

(Magic—you know what magic is, don't you? Some people call it prayer. Some call it grace. Some call it hypnosis. It's all the same. It all comes from the same source: a sort of Van Allen Belt of power. Anyone can tap into it. Anyone can use it—for good or evil. You think I am making this up, but I'm not. I really believe this. Vange really believed this.)

A couple of days later, on a Sunday, I was riding the bus alone, and Old Grumpy was driving. I was on the long side seat, by the front of the bus, and all of a sudden—hey, a miracle!—Old Grumpy spoke to me.

I helped a girl move yesterday, he said. His voice was full of pride and bewilderment. It was my day off, so I helped her to move.

Well, I was completely flummoxed.

Who? I said. What girl? A friend?

A girl who was on my bus, he said.

No, not a friend.

Just a girl. My wife is very mad at me, he said. That I would give my day off to a stranger....

How did...uh...how did that...uh...happen....

I said.

I mean, I was astounded.

There I was, he said. At the end of the day. It was my last run before I could go home. I was driving to the garage, first to 85th, and then....

She was crying, this girl, and I asked her what was the matter, and she said she'd been kicked out of her apartment, she had to be out the next day, and her brother said she could move in with him for a while, but he worked a double shift on Saturdays, he couldn't help her move....

Hey, this was a major oration for O. G.

What could I do? he said, staring at me, his eyes begging me for an answer. She was *on my bus,* and she was desperate...*she was on my bus....*

He turned his face back to the road, sat, writhed, coughed, hawked phlegm into a kleenex, twisted in an agony of bafflement and pride at his incomprehensible act.

Honestly—this happened; well, I don't know that he was proud, but it seemed to me that he was.

So maybe Al Gore's quest is not hopeless. Maybe the human being can be helped to be good.

We can pray for it. It would take a change in the heart, and I know from my own experience that such things are possible.

I will quote an old friend, Anthony, dead now, who was one of a crowd of people who were trying to force their way through the

doors of a bus in NYC, and he was pushed out of line by a screaming old lady: "Oh, look, lady, we're all on the same bus...."
Said Anthony.

*

Folks. Look. We are all on the same bus.

This book—and all of the author's other books—
may be obtained at Amazon.com, Barnes and Noble,
Infinity Publishing [(877) BUY-BOOK], and some local
bookstores, such as Common Good Books, and
Royal Grounds Coffee Shop.

Anyone wishing to comment may contact the
author
at
number1giraffe@hotmail.com